Sunshine and Shadows

SUNSHINE AND SHADOWS

Lynn A. Glenn

iUniverse, Inc.
New York Bloomington

Sunshine and Shadows

Copyright © 2009 by Lynn A. Glenn

All rights reserved. No part of this book may be used or reproduced by any means, graphic, electronic, or mechanical, including photocopying, recording, taping or by any information storage retrieval system without the written permission of the publisher except in the case of brief quotations embodied in critical articles and reviews.

Disclaimer:

This is a work of fiction. All of the characters, names, incidents, organizations, and dialogue in this novel are either the products of the author's imagination or are used fictitiously.

iUniverse books may be ordered through booksellers or by contacting:

iUniverse
1663 Liberty Drive
Bloomington, IN 47403
www.iuniverse.com
1-800-Authors (1-800-288-4677)

ISBN: 978-1-4401-3762-4 (pbk)

ISBN: 978-1-4401-3763-1 (ebk)

Printed in the United States of America

iUniverse rev. date 4/14/2009

Dedication:

I would like to dedicate this book to my family and my readers. I sincerely appreciate all of the compliments and encouragement I have received from all of you.

Acknowledgements:

I would like to thank, Nancy Felknor and Retha (Billie) Hawley, for the time and effort they spent editing this book. Your expertise was invaluable.

Chapter One

Samantha sat in solitude, dangling her long legs off the dock. Her bare feet splashed in the cool water as she swished them back and forth, sending ripples across the mirror-like surface of the lake. Leaning against the metal pipe that served as a brace holding the dock, she tipped her head to the side and rested it against the hard, cool surface of the metal. Overcome with weariness of mind and body, she closed her eyes and took a deep cleansing breath.

Today had been one of many when she wondered if she could continue the path she had chosen. She felt as if there was no way out of her dark thoughts; no end to the days of hard work ahead of her. Only her motto of 'one day at a time' had gotten her this far, that and her daughter. Five-year-old Paige was the ray of light that kept her searching for peace and normality.

She still wondered if moving back to her parents' resort was the way to go. After holding out for almost two years, she heeded the constant urging of her parents and made the momentous decision. Leaving the security of a good job in Minneapolis, she hoped to make a home in northern Minnesota that would provide Paige with the extra attention she now required.

The death of her husband two years ago still gave her nightmares, and she could tell by Paige's behavior that it had affected her deeply as well. She had become more troublesome in her pre-school class and suffered unusual mood swings. Sam couldn't justify leaving her in a daycare again for this summer.

Rocky had been a devil-may-care, free spirit in his short life. Maurice Stone had been her husband for six years. Even his nickname, "Rocky," came from a fight in high school. His buddies tagged him with it in reference to the boxing movie, but it stuck for good when they realized it fit so perfectly with his last name.

Their years together had been full of turmoil, strife, and worry. A four-wheeler trip with his buddies had ended with him wrapped around a tree, dead on the spot.

Now, because of his irresponsible decisions, she was left with memories, not the best of memories, and a daughter to raise on her own. The premise of moving up here was so she would have help with raising Paige. What it turned out to be, however, was that now she had two elderly parents, a decaying resort, *and* a daughter to manage on her own.

She was so lost in her own thoughts she didn't hear the footsteps behind her.

"Penny for them," a deep voice broke through her musings and brought her back to the present.

The voice was somewhat familiar, and she swung her head in a lazy arc, squinting against the brilliant sun. "Marc?" she said, as her eyes widened. There was no mistaking the familiar hazel eyes and the wide mouth, now softened with lazy humor, crinkling the sun bronzed face. She took in the height and breadth of the man that stood in front of her. "Is that really you?" Her eyes slowly traveled down to his toes, then back up again to his curly, auburn hair. She once again locked onto his gaze. This time there was something deeper, an elusive glint and stillness in his eyes that reached into her very soul. Warmth coursed through her entire body.

Sam took a shaky breath and broke the eye contact. She turned back to concentrate on the bluegill minnows that schooled in the silt of the disturbed waters under her feet. Marcus Hammond had been a neighbor since she was twelve years old. His parents had bought the resort next to the one her parents owned.

The fact that she was five years older didn't seem important back then. His older sister Jessie became her best friend even though a year younger. Jessie didn't like fishing, so it was Samantha and Marc that would take one of the boats and spend quiet hours fishing their favorite haunts together.

"C'mon, whatever put that woebegone look on your face can't be that bad. The sun is shining, the air is fresh, and the loon says the fishing is good." He stepped onto the dock and strolled up next to her.

She felt his hand on her lopsided ponytail as he rubbed the silky, ash blonde strands between his fingers. "Easy for you to say. Your parents have kept the Wilderness Resort in tip-top condition. What are you doing up here away from your city dwellings anyway? They fire you from the cushy job you had in St. Paul?" She glanced up at him again; her hand shielded her dark brown eyes as she faced the sun that haloed his rugged good looks.

"Nope, I quit!"

"You've got to be kidding. Your parents were always bragging about what an important job you had. Even made supervisor from what Mom told me."

"Yeah, well, there were some things missing. I didn't think I'd miss the resort as much as I did. When Mom and Dad asked if I wanted to be a partner, I decided to give it a try. They told me you'd moved back."

She had married Rocky shortly after Marc had graduated from high school, and hadn't kept in touch with Jessie either. They had just drifted apart because Jessie hadn't finished high school yet when Sam left for business school.

She met Rocky several years later while working as an accountant for a prestigious construction company. Rocky was a steelworker; indulging his need for excitement and danger by working on the high, steel girders. He set his sights on Samantha as soon as they met at a company picnic and had commandeered her time and attention from then on.

It was hard to believe she had just passed her thirtieth birthday. It was also hard to believe that Marc's close proximity and his touch on her hair was actually making her extremely aware of him as man.

A dew of perspiration appeared on her brow. She stuck out her lower lip and gave a puff of breath to cool her flushed face. The burst of air lifted her feathery bangs but did little to cool her off. What on earth was the matter with her? This was her fishing buddy, Marc!

"Mom!"

The panic in her daughter's voice drove any other thoughts from her mind. Marc's hand came out to steady her as she jumped to her feet.

"Paige, I'm over here!"

She started jogging towards the excited voice, Marc followed more slowly, wondering if he was intruding.

He stopped as a tornado of short, flying arms and legs came barreling around cabin three. Sam dropped to her knees and caught Paige as she flung herself into her open arms.

"Whoa, baby! What's the matter?" She uttered in a quavering voice.

"I saw him again!" Dark brown eyes were as big as saucers and unshed tears pooled in the corners. Paige's face was white and the freckles covering her nose and cheeks stood out in speckled relief.

"Who did you see?"

"I told you before, I saw the shadow man in the woods back by my tree house!" Paige's bottom lip quivered as she held back the tears.

"Honey, Grandpa and I looked all over, and we didn't see any tracks or any sign of someone being there."

"I knew you wouldn't believe me, you never believe me!" She struggled in her mother's embrace. Jerking free, she tore off to the back of the main lodge where the family quarters were located.

Marc stood for a moment digesting the scene he had just witnessed. No wonder Sam had looked so worried when he first noticed her sitting on the dock. She did indeed have a lot on her plate, and her daughter was obviously top priority.

She was still on her knees when he walked up and held out his hand to help her up. "Want to talk about it?"

She allowed him to help her to her feet and looked up at him. Even though she was considered tall, she had to look up to meet his solemn gaze. She looked deep into his hazel eyes. The combined hues of greens and browns reminded her of the camouflage clothes Paige was now into. As their gaze held, she also became more aware that Marcus was now a virile, adult male. Shifting her gaze away, she pulled free and turned toward the lodge.

"She's had problems every since her dad died so suddenly. Sometimes she's belligerent, and then, sometimes she's so frightened she imagines all kinds of things that might happen to her or to me. I'm beginning to wonder if she knows truth from fiction anymore."

"Has a professional seen her?"

"She's had regular sessions with the pre-school's counselor. They thought she had made good progress. It's after we moved up here that these fears of seeing someone have manifested themselves."

"Are you sure they're made up? She really seemed to think she saw someone." Marc couldn't forget the fear in the child's eyes as she came flying around the corner. He didn't know a whole lot about kids, but could have sworn the fear was warranted.

"Dad and I have searched the woods behind the resort. It's hard to see tracks in last year's leaves, but we didn't notice anything. Anything's possible I guess. I'll just make sure she doesn't go out there to play for a while. I'm sorry Marc, but I have to go in and sort this out. It's so good to see you again, I'm glad you're staying." Her dark eyes avoided his. She also had to sort out those feelings that had assailed her when she had been drawn into the deep, murky depths moments ago.

I'm glad too," he said softly. "Just remember, I'm right next door if you need me."

"Thanks, I've got so much to do before fishing opener I'm sure I'll be kept too busy to think straight." Her despondency was evident in the defeated slump of her shoulders and the crestfallen look on her face.

"My folks and I are almost ready, I'll stop over and help when I can." There was no way he was staying away now that he'd seen her again. Old feelings had re-emerged that needed exploring. He thought the crush he'd had on her for years had been permanently put to rest; now he wasn't so sure. As he studied her profile he could read the worry emanating from her and he was determined to help. The extra resort work he could handle but what about a troubled child? He had no experience in that area.

George and Mary Randall were Samantha's parents. They were

presently studying her over a glass of iced tea as they sat at the large wooden table in the private dining area off the kitchen of the lodge. They had been in their early thirties when Samantha was born. It was a blessing then, but now that they had talked Sam and Paige into returning, they found the stress of having family around constantly, physically and mentally draining.

"Just what did Paige say she saw this time?" John questioned as he took a sip of the amber tea.

"She's mad at me so didn't want to talk much, but I got out of her that her mysterious stranger had a long coat and a hat pulled down over his face." Samantha drew her hand over her face. "I can't tell if it was really a person or someone she was describing out of a video or comic book. Who around here would wear a long coat and a hat? Mostly it's jackets and baseball caps or fishing hats."

"Have you mentioned any of these stories to Rocky's parents? Maybe Sally and Jack would have some clue as to Paige's behavior," Mary questioned.

She was short and plump and her hair short and frizzy from a recent perm. A home dye job left it auburn with an orange tint. Dark brown eyes searched Samantha's face. She thought Sam was finally getting over losing her husband but now it was obvious that something was disturbing Paige. When she had talked Sam into coming home with Paige she hadn't anticipated being involved in all of this drama.

"I haven't called them lately. I tried to keep them involved after Rocky's accident, but it was as though Paige and I reminded them of his death. They never did approve of our marriage, but they seemed to come around after Paige was born." Sam shrugged her shoulders and looked at her mother. "It really got weird though after Rocky died. Every time I called they made some excuse not to see us. I finally just gave up. I gave them our address when we moved and figured they can find us if they want to."

"We'll just have to put a concentrated effort into keeping an eye on her," John stated. He was tall and thin but no matter how much Mary fed him he stayed as lean as a beanpole. A shock of snow-white hair made him look even older than he was. His penetrating, deep blue eyes looked concerned as he twirled his glass in the puddle of condensation.

Deep lines furrowed his brow, and his bushy eyebrows nearly met as he pulled them in, focused on the conundrum Paige presented.

"I'm going to go up and get her. She can help me paint the frames on the window screens so we can put them on the cabins tomorrow. If we can keep her busy, maybe it will keep her mind off whatever's bothering her."

Sam hoped so anyway as she climbed the narrow stairs to the loft above. "Hey buddy, I need some help outside." She vowed not to mention the scare again, hoping Paige would talk to her when she was ready.

"Hi, Mom. I'm in my bedroom. What'cha gonna do?"

Sam gave a sigh of relief. Her daughter sounded back to normal. She was usually a fun loving kid. They had a lot of fun times and giggle sessions before their lives had been turned upside down.

She sat down next to Paige on the bed that had once been hers. They had re-decorated. Now, instead of the pink and frilly furnishings Mary had preferred, it was now a jungle theme with monkeys, lions and giraffes frolicking along the borders. The dormer windows overlooked the lake and were now adorned with curtains made out of camouflage netting, picked out by Paige. Sam re-arranged a stuffed menagerie as she continued her conversation.

"We're going to pull the screens off the older cabins and paint them. Then, tomorrow, we'll have the fun job of putting them all back on again."

"That's what you call fun?" The sarcasm was softened by the grin on Paige's face.

The rest of the afternoon consisted of scraping off the peeling paint and repainting. It was obvious that it hadn't been done in a long time. The cabins themselves were varnished logs and, although they needed work too, they didn't look as bad as the windows. There were four more modern cabins but the three they were working on were from the original resort, and although they had been modernized, they still retained the old, rustic appeal.

Paige dug right in, and Sam could tell her daughter felt really grown up when she got to wield the paintbrush by herself. Even though it took extra time with the clean up, it was worth it seeing her little helper concentrating on the job of keeping the paint on the wood, not the mesh. She watched as Paige's little tongue stuck out the side of her mouth as she focused on the important job entrusted to her.

It was a tired, dirty, and paint spattered pair that called it a day just as the sun set over the opposite shoreline. They stopped for a moment to appreciate the pink and coral streaks that shot up from the horizon. The colors of sky and trees were mirrored in the calm surface.

"Wow Mom, look at that! We didn't see that when we lived in the city."

"No we didn't. I'm sure it was there, just hidden behind the tall buildings and fuzzy with smog. Do you like it that we moved up here?"

Paige hesitated a moment too long before she answered, and Sam regretted the question.

"Yah mom, I guess I do. I really liked working with you today and I like it that you're always home and I don't have to go to the daycare lady."

Samantha dropped down and put her arms around her daughter as she placed a kiss on the sweaty forehead. Paige was getting old enough so she didn't always allow shows of affection, but this time she wrapped white speckled arms around her mom. "I like it too!" Sam whispered, "I like it a lot!"

It was two days before the paint was dry enough to put the windows back up. Once again Paige was helping as much as she could. Sam was on the ladder precariously balancing the screen that Paige had shakily hefted up to her. It was uncommonly hot for this early in the spring, and she had dug out her torn off denim shorts and tank top for the job. Still, sweat was dripping into her eyes, and she ineffectively wiped her brow on her forearm.

Only her daughter's presence curbed the words that were on the tip of her tongue as she tried pounding the swollen wood back into the original space.

"I told you to call me if you needed help." There was censure in the familiar voice.

Sam became motionless and closed her eyes "*Oh no!*" she thought. "*Why did I wear these short shorts?*"

Marc also stood motionless awaiting her response. He swallowed several times as he gazed at the slim, tanned expanse of legs. His eyes followed them up until the hint of rounded cheeks that peeked from under the frayed denim were right at eye level. His gaze continued up to the short tank top that had ridden up to reveal a trim waist and was stretched taut over generous breasts. So much bare skin dared him to touch and see if it was as smooth as it appeared. Taking a shaky breath, he managed to find the control needed to stop himself as he stepped back.

Turning to face Paige, who was gazing at him warily, he said, "Do you and your mom need some help? By the way, my name's Marc." He stuck his hand out waiting to see if the belligerent look would stay in place.

Paige hesitated a moment but then took the offered hand thinking it was something grownups did, and she liked being treated like a grown up. She slid a questioning glance up at her mom before saying, "Hi, I'm Paige, maybe you can help get that window in. She's gettin' kind of mad at it. I can tell 'cause she's all red and mumbling stuff I can't hear."

Marc glanced back up at Sam. "I noticed that when I walked up. I think she's even redder now." A mischievous grin crinkled his eyes as he craned his neck around so he could look her in the face.

The glare he received back changed his grin into a wide smile as he laid his hand on the ladder close to the tempting thigh.

The move didn't go unnoticed by Samantha. She gave one more whack at the window, which secured it enough so she could let go, but still didn't seat it in completely.

"Okay, if you're so sure you can do it better, have at it." She quickly backed down the ladder and gestured towards it with a sweeping motion of her hand.

As he stepped forward and climbed the ladder, it was her turn to admire a narrow waist and really cute tush under the tight jeans. Her eyes rose to take in the broad shoulders encased in a faded blue tee shirt. The sleeves had been ripped out and showed sleek muscles and sinewy forearms covered with golden hair.

She couldn't believe the changes that had taken place in her neighbor since she'd been away. Her mom had told her he had been at Rocky's funeral with his family, but everything about that day was still a blur in her memory.

A few sound thuds with the side of a firm fist sank the frame of the screen back into the window casing. Marc looked down at her with a smirk and raised eyebrows, but knew better than to say anything. The disgusted look on her face said it all.

"Go ahead, say what you're thinking or you'll burst," Sam said. "Just try and make some remark about needing a man around the place and I'll thump you like you thumped those windows."

"Why, Samantha, I'd never have made that assumption; funny the thought would come to *your* mind. Here I came to the aid of a damsel in distress and all I get is threats of physical abuse." Stepping down from the ladder he turned to Paige with a smile that would melt butter. "Now, what do you think your mother should do young lady? What are you supposed to do when someone helps you out?"

"Mom tells me I'm s'pose to say "thank you," don't you Mom?" Paige's smile was uncommonly close to the one that was still plastered on Marc's face.

Samantha solemnly looked from one countenance to the other. "I think I'm being ganged up on here. My own daughter's taken the other side." She faked a punch at her daughter's tummy, then grabbed her and twirled her in a circle. "Okay, okay," she turned to Marc with Paige still gripped to her side. "Thank you very much sir," she said primly, which brought another giggle from Paige.

"You're very welcome, Madam." Marc gave a sweeping bow, one hand across his chest and the other one extended.

"Oh, cut it out," Sam laughed, "I think this has gone on long enough, I really appreciate the help."

"Well, that's better. Let's get the rest of these screens on, then I'll help get the boats ready. I saw your dad working on the motors in the garage when I came. I told him I would help you get the boats cleaned up and we can put the motors on later, when he has them ready. When that's done, I'll help you get them in the water."

"Marc, we really don't need you to do all of this work, we'll get it done." She couldn't keep the doubt out of her voice, but it didn't feel right to have him putting so much time in when she knew there was probably something he could be doing at his own place.

"But, Mom! Grandma was just telling you she didn't think Grandpa could do such heavy work much longer. I heard her when you were in the kitchen."

"Paige," Samantha said, drawing the name out in a warning tone, "Marc has a place of his own to run. We can manage this one."

"Out of the mouths of babes," they say. Come on Sam, let me help," Marc pleaded soberly. "You can make it up to me when things ease up a bit; anyone can see you're running yourself into the ground."

Samantha's insecurity sent her temper flaring. "And what's that supposed to mean? Sorry I don't come up to your standards, but it's been a long time since I've had the time, or inclination, to fix myself up. What you see is what you get!" No, she instantly knew, that came out wrong. He never said he wanted to get *her*. Why did that thought pop into her mind? She clamped her mouth shut and slanted a glance up at him.

He stood perfectly still. His somber eyes caught and held hers; neither of them blinked for a long moment. "Well now, there's a thought," he murmured softly.

"Yeah! Right!"

"Mom! I'm hungry, you said we could eat after the windows were up, and they aren't ever gonna' get up if you just stand there. Let Marc help 'cause my tummy is really, really hungry."

"Alright, you guys win. Paige, you can go to the kitchen and ask Grandma if you can have a snack. Marc and I will finish these before I come in." A glance back at him caught a satisfied smile, and something deeper going on in those hazel eyes. She shrugged it off as her imagination.

No more was said of the conflict as the rest of the screens were replaced with a minimum of effort that left Samantha torn between resenting the ease with which he managed it, and yet marveling at the ease in which he managed it.

As they worked together, Marc noticed that she avoided being close to him. Whenever he moved closer, she found something that would give her a reason to move away. The fact that his presence evidently bothered her made him wonder why. He knew why her close proximity bothered him; he'd been living with the attraction for years.

Now, he thought he would pursue the reason for the tension he could feel crackling in the air. With a grin lifting one corner of his wide mouth, he deliberately invaded her space whenever she moved away. He didn't make any overt moves that she would recognize, just nonchalantly nudged a little bit closer than necessary when taking a screen from her or moving the ladder.

Samantha couldn't figure out why Marc was constantly brushing against her or breathing down her neck. Was he doing it deliberately, or was she just unusually aware of his nearness?

She slanted a quick glance his way and he caught her eye, but the innocent look he sent her made her think she was making more of the moves than was necessary. Still, she became jittery each time he got within a few feet of her.

His male, musky, workingman odor assailed her senses and had her breathing deep breaths to capture his unique scent. She could feel the warmth emanating from him, heating her already flushed face.

When he was turned away, her eyes couldn't help but turn to admire the breadth of firm shoulders and strength of muscled thighs. She immediately shifted her gaze when he turned towards her.

Marc almost burst out laughing when he caught her eyeing his behind. "*Oh, Samantha,*" he thought, "*This is going to be an interesting summer.*" He knew what her reaction would be if he revealed his interest right now. Slow, easy and determined was going to be his game plan. He knew from her reactions that she was going to resist the age difference, but to him they were both adults and the years were no longer an issue.

Several days later, Marc sat at the breakfast table sipping a cup of steaming coffee with his parents, John and Peggy. He and his father were discussing all of the things that needed to be done before the opener. At this time of year that was all that was on resort owners' minds. Opening of fishing season was almost a holiday in the resort community.

"I'm going to put the boats in today, Dad. I'll take each out for a spin to see how the motors are running. If they're all in working order, I think I'll drop over to Pine Shores and see if they need any help."

John sent an amused glance toward his son. "How come you're so interested in helping out our competitors all of a sudden?" He was a huge man with a ruddy complexion and a sparkle in his dark brown eyes. There were signs of gray hair filtering through the dark brown, closely cropped curls. Laugh lines creased his weathered face from the frequent smiles that were a part of his demeanor. There was a lot of teasing and horseplay in the family. No one was immune to good-natured ribbings and practical jokes.

Peggy also had the glimmer of a smile on her face as she slanted a quick glance at her son. She was a match for her husband in the wit department and held her own in their frequent arguments. Her red hair and green eyes attested to her Irish heritage, and her petite build belied the strength of mind and body.

Both she and her husband had been acutely aware of the infatuation their son had on Samantha as a teenager. They'd even kidded him about it when he was young, but stopped years ago when it was obvious the teasing had become hurtful to a sensitive adolescent.

She could have sworn Marc had gotten over his teen-age crush, because for years he didn't even mention her or make an effort to contact the family when she came home on her infrequent visits. They knew he'd had several girlfriends, but none he'd ever brought home.

Now, she could read something different about him, a subdued excitement, as though he was holding a deep secret. Her mother's intuition made her hope that whatever his intentions, he didn't get hurt.

She'd always liked Samantha and enjoyed the years when the kids had been in and out of both households. They felt the loss long after Sam graduated and moved away. Neither she nor John had approved of Samantha's choice of a husband and only saw them briefly after the marriage.

"Well, Dad, I'm just being neighborly," Marc said with a half-smile of his own. His voice became serious as he looked up into his dad's eyes. "They're having trouble getting ready. I don't know why George and Mary have let that place go downhill. Sam's working herself sick trying to get caught up and is worried about her little girl to boot."

"What's wrong with her daughter?" Peggy questioned, her brows furrowed in concern.

"I don't really know. I was there the other day when she came screaming that she saw somebody in the woods. She plays in that old tree house of Sam's and swears she saw someone watching her. The look on her face convinced me that she either saw someone or thought she did. She was scared to death. Her eyes were as big as saucers when

I first saw her. I just wanted to pick her up and hold her to keep her safe."

"I haven't seen Sam's little girl for years. How old is she now?" Peggy pondered.

"I think she's about five and Sam said she's been having trouble since her dad died." Marc's voice softened. "Mom, she's the cutest little kid you've ever seen. She has big brown eyes with thick black, curly eyelashes. Her hair is dark and curly and in a messy pony tail like her mom's."

He was gazing into the dregs at the bottom of his coffee cup as he remembered the little girl so missed the knowing glance that was exchanged between his parents. Their gaze locked and held for a long moment as if to say "Oh! Oh! here we go again!"

"Maybe we should check out the woods ourselves. That's heavily wooded land that runs behind our resort and theirs. I don't like the thought of someone lurking around that we don't know about. A lot of our guests have little kids, and the idea that they might be in danger worries me." John was serious as he voiced his concern.

"I already did a preliminary search," Marc said. "I did find where the leaves had been disturbed close to the tree house. I just couldn't tell if it was human footprints or animal. The squirrels and deer have been digging up last year's acorns so there were patches of messed up soil and overturned, dead vegetation all over. The problem we have, according to Sam, is whether to believe Paige or not. She's worried that it might all be in her imagination brought on by the trauma of losing her dad." Worry lines creased Marc's tanned brow as he continued to swirl the coffee remains in his mug.

Peggy read the concern in her son's face. "I'm glad that we're aware of the situation and I suggest we don't say anything to anyone, just keep our eyes and ears open. Be more vigilant and observant than before, but go on as normally as we can. It won't do anyone any good to start a panic, and if there is someone around we'll be more apt to discover them if they don't know we're watching."

"Thanks, you guys. I didn't know whether to tell you about this or not. It might be nothing to worry about. I just have a weird feeling about it. Now, I've got to get busy. You too, old man." He punched his dad in the shoulder and received a quick feint back as they all rose from the table.

Peggy was somber as she watched the two men, so much alike, slam the screen door on their way out. She shook her head with a resigned smile. How many times had she told them to shut the door and not let it slam? She could tell by her son's behavior that he was going to be drawn into Sam's world again, and hoped he had gained enough maturity to weather the turbulence she predicted was going to be in his future. The fact that he mentioned Sam, only in reference to the little girl, set off warning bells in her mother's intuition. She knew he was struggling with his latent infatuation and wasn't ready to talk about it to his parents yet.

Chapter Two

What a beautiful little girl. I would love to run my fingers through that shiny hair. She really is observant. Too bad she caught a glimpse of me. I must be more careful.

Her mother must have told the neighbors, they've been snooping all around the woods. It's a good thing they didn't find anything. I haven't seen them lately so they must have given up and maybe they'll forget about it now.

I just want to touch her; her skin looks soft, so soft. I must be careful, I must be more careful. I just have to be close to her.

Chapter Three

"Dad, why won't Mom let me help her with the books? She's always struggling and muttering about them, but when I offer to help, she guards them jealously as if I'm trying to take her job away." Samantha questioned her dad as they were working on a boat motor that was being stubborn about starting. "I've had the training, and maybe I could figure out an easier way to manage the accounting end of it. I've got the software on my computer, and it wouldn't take any time to set up a program. We've got to start hiring soon and it would be much simpler if the payroll was done electronically."

"I don't know, Sam. She won't let me near them either. I've offered to help, and in fact, I would like to know more about what comes in and goes out of the business. I hate having to ask her for something I need for the resort. Half the time she says we don't have the money for it. Whenever I ask to help she treats me the same way, like I don't trust her or something." He wiped his greasy hands on a well-used rag as he turned to her. "Tell you what, she always goes to play bingo on Wednesday nights. We'll check out the books then - after all, it's my resort too, and soon to be yours. I think we should know where we stand before this season starts."

Wednesdays were always a big day for Mary. She started preparing for her evening out right after lunch and her excitement was obvious to the rest of the family. Paige tried to talk to her and was brushed off with an, "I'm too busy today to watch you, go play outside."

Sam could never understand how anyone could get so worked up over a bingo game. She remembered her mother occasionally going out to play but never to the extent she did now. There was nothing that could get in the way of her night out, family or business matters could wait, but her bingo games couldn't.

This Wednesday was no different. She left the lodge in a flutter of fluffed hair, too much make-up, and a cloud of some flowery fragrance wafting after her. Sam watched her go in amazement. She shook her head as her mother's Buick left a dust trail down the winding driveway. She sat down at the table to play a board game with Paige until her dad came in.

"This can't be right!" Samantha looked up at her father in awe. She was sitting at a beat up old wooden desk that had been a part of the room for as long as she could remember. The bookkeeping books that Mary kept well out of sight in a filing cabinet were spread out in front of her. "This resort can't possibly have spent this much money and still be as rundown as it is."

Turning the books so her dad could see, she pointed out the expenditures that were written out weekly. Most of the checks were accounted for as legitimate bills for the usual electricity, heating, groceries, insurance, etc., but every week there was a five hundred dollar check made out to 'cash'.

George looked at the figures, then turned page after page backwards. Sure enough, once a week there was the same unexplained withdrawal. There was pain in his eyes as he looked over at his daughter. "All of those checks were made out on a Wednesday."

"Dad, that's two thousand dollars a month! Those rotten windows on the cabins could have been replaced with that kind of money! You could have some new boats or motors instead of trying to patch up those old tubs."

"There must be some explanation, we'll just have to ask your mother when she gets home. Maybe she put it in savings or something." Disbelief was evident in his voice and his face was haggard and lined. He couldn't believe his wife could have been deceiving him and he not known about it.

Samantha's gut was tied in a knot as she lay in bed with her arm flung over her eyes, listening for her mother's return. She didn't want to believe what she had just witnessed, but knew enough about accounting to detect the inconsistencies immediately. These withdrawals were so blatant they weren't even hidden under some other account. It was evident now why her mother was so possessive of the ledgers she hoarded. Sam dreaded the confrontation she knew was coming. "What did I get into by coming home?" she asked herself. It seemed one conflict after another was destined to follow her.

She had fallen into a restless sleep, but was awakened by the sound of her mother's car at two o'clock in the morning. There were no voices or commotion so she assumed her father had fallen asleep, and the altercation she expected was going to be postponed until tomorrow. She wondered how she was going to be able to shield Paige from the upcoming brouhaha. Paige had seen and heard more than her share of conflicts in her young life. Sam couldn't justify letting her get involved in another.

Her question was answered the next morning. Nervously waiting for her mother to get up after her late night, Sam took Paige for a walk along the beach. Later they planned on preparing the flowerbeds for the bedding plants. The day was dark and threatening, but she hoped the rain would hold off until evening. The lake was steel gray, white caps on each rolling wave tumbled toward shore and crashed fruitlessly on the sand. A rim of dirty white froth flowed and ebbed along the shifting beach.

Both she and Paige wore windbreakers with the hoods pulled up to protect their ears from the wind. Paige's was red with a white lining and hers was white with red trim. They were swinging held hands as they strolled along, eyes on the pebbles at their feet to see if they could spot an agate.

Agate hunting had been a pastime of Sam's since she had been introduced to the hobby of collecting the beautifully striped stones. Paige picked up on the obsession and they both watched with intensity as they moseyed down the beach, occasionally picking one up to examine it and either discarding it or tucking it into a pocket.

Marc watched them moving towards him as they wandered from their resort to his. He couldn't describe the intense feeling as they moved closer, still with downward cast eyes. What a beautiful sight!

How would he be able to hide his feelings while they got to know him and trust him?

As they approached, he couldn't help but notice the haunted look that was again in Samantha's eyes. Outwardly, she looked relaxed as she discussed the rocks with her daughter. He, however, could read the inner expressions that she was so good at hiding.

"Well, well, what have we here? I do declare, it's trespassers I'm a seein'," he drawled.

Both Sam and Paige's eyes flew upward. Sam quickly glanced back down the beach unaware of how far they had walked. Paige, on the other hand, broke into a big smile. "Hi, Marc," she said, digging into her jacket pocket. "Look what I found all by myself. Look at the lots of lines. Mom calls them ribbon agates 'cause they're striped like ribbons. I like the red ones and she likes the creamy colored ones. Which do you like the best?"

Marc dug deep into a jeans pocket that was so tight only his fingers could reach the bottom and produced a beautifully striped agate much larger than any they had. "I have this one, but I like yours a lot better. Do you want to trade?"

"Wow, that's big! You sure you want mine? It's a lot littler."

"I'm sure. I have a collection it will fit into better than this big thing." He held out the rock and she took it, turning it over in her small hand.

"Look, Mom. It's humongous! Thanks Marc!" Paige turned the rock over and licked it, because any agate hunter knows the lines stand out better when wet, then tucked it in a special pocket of her camouflage pants.

"Did you know a kind of agate is Minnesota's state rock?" Marc asked Paige.

"State rock? I didn't know there was a state rock. I know the loon is the state bird, Mommy told me that. We heard a loon this morning, didn't we Mom?" At a nod from her mother she continued. "And I know the state flower is the pink lady slipper, don't I Mom? But I've never seen those. Only pictures in a book Mommy showed me. She said she's never seen them either. I wonder why they're the state flower when no one can even find one?" She pondered this dilemma while Marc watched, entranced by the little munchkin.

Samantha had been watching with a half smile. When her eyes caught his she mouthed the words, "Thank you."

He shrugged the thanks off, "My pleasure," he whispered back. "What do you ladies have planned for today?" he questioned.

"We're just killing some time, getting some fresh air," Samantha said with a smile. Her voice was strained as though forcing her good-natured reply.

"Killing time this early in the day?" Marc said softly, looking at her closely. Something was going on. As usual he didn't have a clue as to what was upsetting her this morning, but instinctively knew something was wrong.

She raised her chin and met his gaze. How could he read her so well? It was as if she was transmitting her thoughts and he was receiving them. Why did he act as if he knew how troubled she was? Why did he care?

"As long as you're killing time how about coming in and seeing Mom and Dad. They've been asking about you and Paige. Looks like you could both do with some hot chocolate. Your noses are as red as Rudolph's." He tweaked Paige's button nose with his fingers. "Look, I stole your nose!" he said, showing the tip of his thumb between his index and middle finger.

"Mom does that all the time!" Paige giggled. "Mom, can I have some hot chocolate?"

Samantha was torn between not wanting to encourage Marc and not wanting to return to the conflict between her mother and father. She longed for her own place; somewhere she could curl up and lick her wounds. The thought of taking Paige and running away was sometimes overwhelming. Only the thought of her daughter kept her grounded.

Marc watched the emotions flit across Sam's expressive face. If only he knew the source of the sorrow and fear he saw there, maybe he would know how to proceed in eradicating them. "Well?" he encouraged.

"Okay, you two always get your way, know that?" she capitulated. "I think you're both spoiled!"

Paige and Marc grinned at each other and completed at 'high five', one chubby, grubby little five, and one lean, tanned big five.

Peggy and John looked up from some papers they had spread out on the table as the door opened. Expecting Marc, they couldn't conceal their surprise as he ushered the girls in before him.

"Why, Samantha, it's so good to see you again! I've been wanting to get over to see you ever since I heard you were back." Peggy jumped to her feet to encase Sam in a bear hug.

Her enthusiasm was infectious, and John had to pull her away with a, "my turn," to wrap his arms around Sam. He pulled her into his massive chest and lifted her off her feet as he swung her around. "Hey, Sampson, it's been way too long since you stood in this kitchen." He used the nickname he had given her when they first moved here.

Sam was overwhelmed with emotion as tears welled in her expressive, brown eyes. She felt so safe as she was held and cuddled in the arms of her friend. She had truly felt a part of this family years ago before her life had started to fall apart. She wanted to stay in the warm embrace and be taken care of. A quick glance through her tears caught the eyes of another observing the reunion. Why did all of a sudden it feel as though it was his arms that comforted her, his warmth that enfolded her?

Marc's serious, expressive eyes caught and held hers as he tried once more to delve into the reason for her repressed emotions. He wished he had the right to change places with his uninhibited father. He would give anything to have her relax in his arms and hug him back. "*Soon*," he told himself, "*Soon*."

"Let go my mom!" Paige pushed herself between her mother and John with a frown on her face. She wasn't used to such unrestrained enthusiasm. Other than her mom, the other grown ups in her life had been reserved in showing their affection. Even her dad hadn't done more than give her a kiss and quick hug now and then.

Marc was the first to step forward. "Whoa! Paige, it's all right," he soothed as he knelt beside her. "This is my dad, and that lady there with the red hair is my mom. We've all known your mommy for years, and they're just showing her how much they missed her. No one here is going to hurt her or you. You're always going to be safe with us," he promised. He looked deep into the soft brown eyes, so like others he couldn't get out of his mind. "You trust me, don't you?"

After a long look at him and then at her mom, she nodded her head and her ponytail bounced. She then looked up at John, who stood unusually quiet while she gave him close scrutiny. As her eyes reached his, he winked, and all of a sudden a smile lit up her face that reached the heart of every adult there.

"How about that hot chocolate?" Marc scooped her up as he rose to his feet. "Mom, got any of that hot chocolate you keep in the cupboard? I promised these wanderers we could get them warmed up before we let them walk back home."

Samantha observed the scenario that took place before her eyes in amazement. Marc had stepped to her daughter's aide before she could catch her breath. In a matter of seconds, he had reassured Paige and had everyone back on comfortable grounds. She glanced at the man holding her daughter so naturally and met the laughing eyes. With a wink similar to his father's, he had her grinning back and shaking her head. This was the most natural family she had ever met.

After the whole family participated in an impromptu snack of hot chocolate and cookies, Sam said they had to be heading home. She secretly hoped she had given her parents enough time to resolve their problem, at least enough time to have cooled off so they wouldn't upset Paige.

"I'll walk you back," Marc offered, pushing back from the table.

"No!" burst out of Sam before she thought. As all eyes turned on her she felt a moment of panic. She couldn't explain why she didn't want anyone to know her family problems. "We'll be okay," she assured them, her face flushed in embarrassment. "Come on Paige, get your jacket on."

Several moments passed in silence after Marc and his parents saw Sam and Paige out the door.

"What the hell is going on with that girl, Son?" John was never one to mince words. "She's as jumpy as a cat on a griddle and that little girl is awfully protective for a kid her age."

"Yes, Marc. Samantha has changed a lot since we've seen her. I expected her to be more mature but she looks too strained and I think there's more than her husband's death bothering her." Peggy laid her hand on his arm. She knew as soon as she saw them together that his feelings for Sam had returned, full force. "Are you sure you want to get involved? Sometimes family matters can be tricky, especially with a young child involved."

Marc took a deep breath and let it out slowly. "Mom, Dad, I don't have a choice. The minute I saw Sam sitting on the dock looking like she expected the world to end, or worse yet, wanted it to end, I knew I didn't have a choice. When I saw the fear in Paige's eyes I knew I didn't have a choice." He laid his hand over his heart and stated simply. "I can't let them go. I know I'm butting in. I know she's going to fight me tooth and nail, but I have to do what I can. I care for her too much to let it go. This time I'm old enough to fight for what I want. I can't let her walk away again."

"It's not going to be easy Son, I respect your feelings but the age difference is only the tip of the iceberg. She's been through a lifetime of experiences you can't even fathom. From the haunted look in her eyes, I can tell there are secrets she's guarding from us, from you." Peggy's green eyes were sad as she held her son's hand. She knew he was going to follow his heart and was afraid it was going to be broken again.

"Hey, Mom, it'll be all right! Nothing's so bad that the Hammond household can't fix it, right? We just have to work together. I figure if she knows she can trust us, she'll open up and I can find out what's really at the root of her fears." He puffed out his chest, threw his shoulders back and hooked his thumbs under his armpits. "She's as stubborn as always so I might have to crank up the charm. I think Paige already likes me, don't you?" With a grin crinkling his eyes and tipping the corners of his mouth, his good humor was back intact.

"You know, you are way too much like your father? He has a whole lot of confidence in his 'charm' too. What ticks me off is that it usually works around here!" With a grin very similar to her son's she swatted his shoulder. "Get busy! If you think you're up to running this resort and the one next door too, you'd better be getting at it."

Sam took her time returning to the resort. Paige had all kinds of questions about the Hammonds and about when her mother used to visit them. Samantha was happy to see her daughter so interested and animated. They had a good conversation that brought back fond memories until they came to the large, carved, wooden pine tree with the name Pine Shores Retreat in front of the lodge.

She was trying to figure out the best way to get Paige up to her room without running into her parents when she noticed her dad out in the garage. Deducing that it would be safe now, she turned to her daughter. "Paige, go up to your room and put some dry shoes on, maybe some dry jeans too. Looks like you got a little too close to the waves. I'll be up in a minute. I have to talk to Grandpa first."

"Well Dad, how did it go?" Samantha leaned against the workbench, careful not to get too close to the greasy motor her dad was working on.

It took a moment for George to answer. The anguished look on his face pretty much told the story. His voice broke when he first spoke and he had to clear his throat and try again. "She's been gambling."

"Gambling?" Sam said in disbelief. "How can you gamble five hundred dollars a week playing bingo?"

"Seems it isn't just bingo. She's been playing the pull-tabs and lottery. Sometimes she and her cronies head to the casinos too. No wonder she gets home so late. Every time she loses she spends more, trying to hit a big one to catch up."

"What are you going to do about it, Dad?"

"I don't know for sure. She's so mad at us for checking the books she's trying to make us out to be the bad guys. She still thinks she can hit a big jackpot and it will end all of our worries. What she won't admit is that we wouldn't have worries if she hadn't spent our capital on her gambling habit."

"Do you think she needs help? There are places gambling addicts can go for counseling now."

"She won't go. She doesn't think she has a problem. I don't know what to do." George looked at her apologetically. "I did tell her you were going to be doing the accounting from now on. I took the checkbook and ledgers; they're over there in that box." He gestured to a cardboard box under the bench. "I'm afraid you're on her blacklist too."

He carefully cleaned his hands with grease cleaner, wiped them on a clean rag and turned to face her. "I'm sorry honey. I know you have enough to worry about without this added to your problems. If you want to go back to the cities I'll understand."

"Dad, I can't go back now. It would be hard for Paige to try and re-adjust again so soon. Even though we've got problems here, I think we have a good chance of working them out."

She looked into her father's bright blue eyes and read the pain, but inexplicably, her memory then flicked to the compassion and kindness of another pair of very dissimilar, hazel eyes.

No, she couldn't leave now, not when she had found a small slice of comfort and hope. Marc had asked to help and for the first time, she gave free rein to the thought that maybe now was the time to pursue that possibility. The immediate rapport he had formed with her daughter was what Paige had been missing. They both needed a friend they could trust. She assured herself it would just be friendship.

The genuine warmth of his family's greeting still sent a glow through her at their generous acceptance. She had forgotten what an open, comfortable, loving family they were. She now knew it was a rarity that should be cherished.

Several mornings later, Samantha and her father were sitting at the table alone. The sun streamed through the multi-paned window and dust moats floated aimlessly in the brilliant shafts of light. She sipped at the steaming cup of coffee, inhaling the rich aroma that she always associated with this kitchen. Her parents always had a pot ready for anyone that stopped in.

Paige wasn't up yet, and Mary had made a point of staying in the bedroom until Sam and George went about the work of the day. Sam was actually surprised they were still sharing a bed from the cold shoulder her dad was receiving.

"How long do you think this is going to last, Dad?" Sam couldn't keep the worry out of her voice as she pushed her plate of congealed eggs aside. Making breakfast wasn't her greatest accomplishment, but since her mother was evidently on strike, she made the attempt. "I tried to talk to Mom and she just gave me a cold stare. We're going to have to start hiring pretty soon. I have the cabins almost ready for the opener, but we still have to get cabin cleaners on deck before then so they are here for the changeover the next weekend." She gave up on eating and stood to clear the table. "We could use the yard boys right now. Since I'm setting up the accounting program, I haven't had time to get at the flowerbeds and there's still raking that has to be done."

George tipped his head back to drain the last of the coffee from his favorite, chipped mug. "I'm sorry, Sam, but it looks like you're going to have to do the hiring this year."

"Me? I've never done that before. Mom has always done it, why can't you?"

"Believe me, hon, you have as much experience in that as I have. That's another area she had control over. Just go over last year's lists and call those women to see if they want to come back. If not, put an ad in the Shorecrest Shopper. All of the locals read it. There are always some people looking for summer jobs." He took one look at the exasperated look on his daughter's face and stood. "You can do it, Sam," he assured her as he headed for the door.

Sam ran her fingers through her long hair and pulled it back from her face in frustration as she tipped her head back and closed her eyes. The muscles in her jaws bulged as she gritted her teeth so hard it hurt. "God, give me strength!" she muttered.

Days of phone calls, interviews, applications, and frustrations filled the next two weeks for Sam. Mary was still stubbornly staying out of everything. She spent hours each day away from the resort, and Sam couldn't help but be suspicious of where she went. George cut her 'bingo' money down to fifty dollars a week after she promised she would only play bingo, and only with her friends at the VFW post.

Finally, Sam had enough employees hired to fill the positions needed. She had two teams of housekeepers that would come in Saturday mornings. One team would clean three cabins and one would clean four. The next week they would exchange to keep it even. She hoped they were as good as they said they were, because there would be a real push to get the cabins cleaned after one group of guests left at ten o'clock in the morning and the new customers came in at one in the afternoon.

The job was familiar to Samantha because she used to be one of the housekeepers when she was in high school. She knew how important it was to have women that worked well together. One would strip sheets and make beds, one would clean the bathroom and another the kitchen. When those were done it was a joint effort to finish up dusting, vacuuming and cleaning windows, then on to the next cabin with no time wasted.

She hired two young men for the landscaping work but told her dad in no uncertain terms that they were his responsibility. She already had too much to do to oversee them.

It had been a particularly grueling day and Sam was exhausted. She had already put a tired and cranky Paige to bed, and although the thought of collapsing in her own bed was appealing, she knew she wouldn't be able to fall asleep this early. Instead, she went for a walk along the beach and returned to her favorite place on the dock to watch the sunset over Shorecrest Lake.

She couldn't count the times she had sat right here and watched the sun recede behind the far horizon. Tonight, Nature was at her finest. The water was as clear as glass, mirroring the topaz and amber streaks that pierced the floating clouds. Darker salmon and pink tipped the trees as the sun slipped out of sight, leaving several more moments of muted beauty.

She turned her head and watched Marc make his way along the shoreline towards her. She quelled the instinct to leave before he got there and waited quietly, watching him approach. Her eyes met his as he slowly moved closer and neither broke the connection until he dropped down beside her. Then her gaze turned to the tips of her shoes.

"Bad day?" Marc's throaty murmur questioned as he reached for her hand. He could see that she had lost weight and there were dark circles under her beautiful eyes. "I'm sorry I haven't gotten over here before this. We had trouble with a boat, then Jessie and her crew came to visit, and I spent some time with them. I would have come to get you to see her but wasn't sure you were ready for that yet. She wanted to come over here but I didn't think that was a good idea either." He reached out a finger to turn her chin so he could look into her eyes. "Was I right?"

"Unfortunately, you're right. I would love to see her though. It's just not a good time around here right now." Sam couldn't keep the quiver out of her voice and was struggling to withhold the tears that were threatening.

"I kinda figured that, the way you left the other day. Is there something you can tell me? I'm a good listener."

Sam hesitated, she really needed to talk to someone, but should she burden him just to make herself feel better?

Marc felt her waver and didn't want her to back out now that they were finally close to talking. "Please, Sam. I know you're having problems. I promise not to interfere if you don't want me to, but just talk to me. It's tearing me up seeing you like this." He raised her clenched hand to his lips and placed his lips on her knuckles. "Please let me in."

"Oh, Marc." Samantha's bottom lip trembled as she looked into the sympathetic eyes. "There's just more than I can handle." A whimper broke through and she tried to turn away.

Marc shifted her away from the edge of the dock and into his arms. He leaned against the post and cuddled her in his lap with his chin resting against her forehead. He could feel her trying to keep from crying and held her tight while slowly rocking her as he would a child. No words were said. He couldn't believe she was allowing him to get this close and wasn't going to mess up by saying the wrong thing.

As Samantha's quiet sobs subsided, Marc could feel her distancing herself. She no longer clung to him with her head buried into his throat, and he could feel the tears on his skin as she lifted her face. He could almost read her mind as she grew still, assessing their positions. "Don't think," he whispered into her hair. "Just relax and enjoy the moment." He was thankful when she took a deep, shaky breath and sunk back against his chest.

They sat like that until the sky was devoid of color and the stars were starting to pierce the canopy above them. "Can you talk about it now?" Marc asked softly. He hated to break the mood, but knew she would leave soon and wanted to see if he could glean some information that might help him understand what was going on.

"Are you sure you want to hear?" Samantha still wasn't convinced she should divulge family discretions.

"I'm sure. I can't help if I don't know what's bothering you, babe." He shifted her so he could watch her face as she talked.

"Dad and I found out why there isn't enough money to keep the resort repaired. Mom's been spending the money on gambling. When he confronted her she got mad and quit working around here." She couldn't keep her voice from breaking as she continued. "I've had to hire all the help while trying to set up an accounting program, do a hundred other things and still keep an eye on Paige so she doesn't wander off." Samantha raised her troubled eyes to look at him. "Marc, sometimes I just don't think I'll make it," she whispered.

Marc felt her pain deep inside his own chest. He wanted to be able to take her home with him, protect her, and take care of her so she never had to worry again. He knew he couldn't. Yet. Right now he could just assure her that he would assist, however she wanted. However much she would allow.

He reached up to cup her face in his big hand; his thumb under her chin. Slowly he lifted her chin and drew her into his smoldering gaze. Never taking his eyes off hers, he lowered his mouth until his lips touched hers in a feathery kiss. As she started to jerk away he tightened his grip on her jaw and raised his other hand to the back of her head, holding her in place.

"I can't let this happen, I can't do this!" was the thought screaming through Samantha's head. She stiffened, but the warm hands holding her gently didn't loosen. Again the soft warmth of his breath touched her lips as he slanted his head and continued the tender nibbling of her sensitive mouth. A shudder went through her as her eyes closed and her lips opened of their own accord.

Suddenly the kiss deepened; the pressure increased as his tongue invaded her welcoming warmth. Her arms reached out to grasp the firm shoulders, and as he shifted his arms to pull her against him, her hands wound themselves in his crisp hair. Their breath mingled as his lips moved over her face and neck to return time and again to plunder her relaxed mouth.

"Oh, Samantha, I've waited so long!" Marc groaned into her mouth. His desire was evident as he pulled her tightly against him.

Reality hit Samantha as Marc's words registered in her fuzzy brain. She tore her mouth away from his and pushed hard on his shoulders as she tried to get away. "Marc, stop! I can't do this!" there was panic in her voice as she jerked backwards.

"Sam, stop it or you're going to end up in the lake!" Marc said as he grabbed for her.

She eluded his grasp and jumped to her feet, but not before he did. He stood between her and the shore and wasn't about to let her leave in this mood. He could tell she wasn't above jumping in the lake so grabbed her by the shoulders and held her.

"Samantha, calm down, we have to talk about this. You must have known how I have felt for years. I can't believe I've read things so wrong as to your interest too. I wasn't the only one involved these last few minutes, so what happened?" He bent his head so he could read her expression. Even though darkness had fallen, the water reflected what light was left, and he could see the panic in her face.

"I'm sorry, Marc. I can't get involved, I've got too many problems to solve. I'm too old for you. I don't know what came over me. I'm sorry," she repeated, tears close to the surface again.

"Samantha, listen to me!" He fought to keep his voice low so she would have to pay attention to hear him. "I'm not going to let you go like this. We have to resolve something here. First of all, *I'm* not sorry! I've loved you for years. I didn't mean to come on so strong, but you drive me crazy. I told myself I would wait until you're ready, until you get to know me again, but I feel your pain and want to help you."

"Marc, just let me go, I'm a mental mess right now, I can't give you what a younger girl can."

"I'm not asking for more than you can give. I'm just asking for a chance, Sam, I've waited years for the few minutes we had tonight. I know you felt something special too. You can't fake a response like that. Just think about it, that's all I'm asking for now."

Samantha looked deep into the beautiful eyes that could read her mind and soul. She searched and found sincerity and what she thought could be love. It was an unknown that she hadn't experienced before. Lust and possessiveness she was well aware of, but to have someone love her, and profess he had loved her for years, was an unknown. Could they really have a future together? She remembered the feel of his mouth on hers, and her body's uninhibited response, but shook away the ghost of hope flitting through her mind.

"I have to go in before they come looking for me," Sam said quietly. "I don't think I can give you what you deserve, Marc. I don't think I can even get my head around the possibility. Getting involved, with anyone, has never entered my mind. Until now," she added with a shaky grin. "You are a really good kisser!" She quickly reached up and pecked him on the cheek before she slipped under his arm and ran to the shore. "G'night Marc!"

Marc stood silently as he watched her run away, physically and mentally. He knew beyond a shadow of a doubt that he wasn't giving up, no matter what excuses she threw at him. He slowly ran his tongue over his lips, cherishing the lingering taste of her. Her response was what he had dreamed of. His response had him hungry for more. He slowly headed towards home; although he had his doubts about how much sleep he would get tonight.

Chapter Four

Fishing season was in full swing by the time Samantha stopped to take a few minutes to herself. It was late afternoon, and she decided to take her daughter out fishing. The guests had all come in from the lake and were doing their various evening rituals. Paige had been getting restless following her around the last few weeks, and she knew she owed both her daughter and herself some time of their own.

"Is this enough, Mommy?" Paige held out a coffee can for her mother to inspect. She was really proud of her accomplishment. Her task for the past few hours was to find enough earthworms for their fishing expedition. It kept Paige occupied and out of Samantha's hair while she finished folding some sheets in the laundry house. If the flowerbeds were a little worse for wear they could be repaired. That was the only place where the dirt was soft enough for little hands with a trowel, to dig.

Sam took a look at the squirmy mass in the bottom of the can and gave her little girl an appreciative smile. "That looks like plenty, you did a great job! Now put a little dirt on them to keep them from drying out. Grab your life jacket, and one for me too, when you go in to wash your hands." She knew washing hands wasn't high on Paige's priority list so reminders were often needed. Not that they would stay clean long in the boat.

"Mom!" Paige gave the usual complaint, but at the raised eyebrows of her mother, she decided this wasn't a good time to argue. Not when the promise of going fishing would be jeopardized! She reluctantly headed out the door.

Sam was in the special building they laughing referred to as – The Outhouse. It was actually the laundry room, built separate from the lodge so they could keep up on the many linens needed for the cabins. The moist, warm air smelled pleasantly of fabric softener and made the hair escaping from her ponytail curl in tendrils around her flushed face.

She was folding the last of the sheets to place in the proper cubbyhole - so the housekeepers wouldn't have any trouble knowing what size and style they were - when she heard a sound behind her. Thinking it was Paige she said sternly, "Paige, if you don't get washed up now we won't have time to go fishing."

"Grandma dear, I brought you a basket of goodies, something you really need! But Granny, you're supposed to be in bed sick, not wrapped up in a sheet." The deep masculine voice forced into a little girl's high pitched sound, made Samantha's lips twitch before she turned around.

"You sound more like the wolf than Little Red Riding Hood."

"But Red, you really should check closer. You don't want to be fooled again!" the voiced changed to a deep throaty growl.

Samantha chuckled as she slowly turned. She held up her hand as Marc started forward. "That's close enough, I don't trust wolves."

"But you haven't checked to see what big teeth I have." Marc said in his own voice. He stopped but the predatory glint in his eye didn't diminish. His hazel eyes flashed with shafts of gold, which enhanced the likeness to the wolf he was emulating.

"It isn't your teeth I'm worried about, Mr. Wolf."

"Worried? About me?" Marc questioned with an angelic look on his face and one hand placed across his heart. "I've never lured an innocent girl into my bed in my life."

"And pigs fly!" Samantha found she was enjoying the lighthearted banter more than she should.

"No, Sam, that's cows that fly, remember? They jump over the moon." He shook his head in exaggerated disappointment.

"Okay, that's enough!" she laughed. "If I'm not mistaken, I'm the one that taught you some of those nursery rhymes." She was still joking, but when she looked up into his face, she saw the humor dissipate. Wondering what she had said that bothered him, she asked, "Mark?"

"Sam?" His question ended there.

"What's wrong, what did I say?" Brown eyes held hazel in a locked embrace.

"Samantha, we were kids. We grew up. I'm a man and you're a woman. I cherish the times we spent together, but now it's going to be different. We can remember the fun times as kids, but please, don't use it as a defense to keep us from moving on. I want an adult relationship now, as I'm pretty sure you're aware of after the evening on the dock."

Samantha's eyes broke contact as she once again studied the toes of her worn deck shoes. "Marc, I tried to explain why I can't! Please don't ask for more than I can give."

Marc stepped forward and drew her into his arms, ignoring the stiffness in her stance. "I'm not, Samantha," he whispered, against her jaw. "I'm just confident you can give. It's just a matter of time, and I have all the time in the world."

He was comforted by the way her body relaxed, and she took a moment to lean into his warm embrace with a shaky sigh. He held her quietly, not asking for more, at least not right now.

The quiet moment was shattered when Paige came running through the door. She was wearing her life jacket but it was undone, strings dangling all around. She was dragging another larger one for her mom, the can of worms clutched to her chest.

Samantha stepped out of Marc's arms, giving his forearms a slight squeeze before she released him. A quick glance at his face showed a sexy smile that made a flush infuse her face.

"Mom! See, I washed my hands!" She held out a still slightly grubby palm for inspection. "Hi, Marc."

She either didn't notice the closeness of the adults, or was beginning to think people hugging her mom was getting to be the norm and it wasn't troubling anymore.

"Hi, Pigeon!"

"It's Paige!" Marc received a condescending look from the pixie face that didn't even come to his waist.

"Paige? Hmm. I like Pigeon. Is it okay if I call you Pigeon and everyone else calls you Paige? That way it will be our special name, just between you and me." Marc knelt in front of her as he spoke. Her dark eyes searched his face as she pondered the question.

"Okay, it'll be our *secret*!" she whispered, leaning forward so her warm breath brushed his ear.

He raised his eyes to watch Samantha's expression as she took in the exchange. What he didn't expect was the tears that welled up in hers.

Wanting desperately to respond to Sam, he instead shifted his attention to Paige. Out of his peripheral vision he saw Samantha turn to compose herself. "What'cha got in the can, Pigeon?"

"I've got worms!" excitement lit up her face as she struggled to get the plastic lid off the coffee can. "Mom let me dig worms in the flower beds. I was careful not to hurt the flowers though," she assured him.

"And what are the worms for?" he said as he stood again.

"Mom and I are going fishing! Right now! Right, Mom?" Paige turned to tug at Samantha's shirttail. "Mom, can Marc go fishing with us?"

Samantha's startled gaze flew from Paige's face to Marc's. The smug look on his face made her squint her eyes and glare at him. When he just grinned and shrugged his broad shoulders, she shook her head, exasperated at his shameless manipulation. "I think Marc has work to do," she said pointedly, watching Marc's response.

He ignored the blatant message and winked at her with another heart stopping smile. "Nope, don't have a thing planned for this evening." He turned to Paige. "Thanks for the invitation Pigeon, I'd love to go fishing with you."

Sam gave them a low throaty growl as she capitulated, once again! "Okay you two, get out of here. Marc, as long as you're so anxious, you can get the boat ready. We'll take the one pulled up on shore. Paige you can grab another life jacket out of the fish cleaning shed for him. Don't forget the worms!" she called after them as they both turned to leave.

Marc and Paige were on the way to the lake. He carried the life jackets; she cradled the precious worms in her arms. "Is my mom mad at us?" she asked, craning her neck to look up at him.

"No, I don't think she's mad, not at you anyway." He laid his free hand on her head; his large hand cupping the side of her face. "Your mom's having some trouble sorting through some grown up things. I think she wanted to go fishing with you alone. Maybe I'm butting in to her plans."

"But Mom and I are together *all* the time." Paige exaggerated. "I think she'll like it that you're there. I like it that you're comin' with." She slanted a quick glance his direction. "Do you put worms on hooks?" she innocently asked.

Marc couldn't help but laugh at the way she slipped that quick question in. At the time she was struggling to get herself and her worms into the fourteen-foot Lund fishing boat. He reached out, ruffled her hair, and gave her a boost onto the middle seat. "I've been known to bait a hook a few times, but your mom always wanted to put her worms on herself. Sure you don't want to do it yourself?"

"I tried once but I got the hook stuck in my finger and Mom had to pull it out." She shook her index finger at him, lowered her voice and said, "Mom said, 'no more hooks until you're older'!"

He was still chuckling over her antics when Samantha joined them. "Just what are you two up to now?" she asked suspiciously. "Every time you two get together I seem to be in trouble."

Marc went to the front of the boat and lifted it with ease as he pushed it further out into the lake. "M'thinks it's you that's the trouble, m'lady," he murmured, as he took her arm to steady her when she stepped into the boat.

His warm touch on her bare skin sent a tingle down to her fingertips and up to her shoulder. She gave a slight shudder as goose bumps covered her satiny forearm and she jerked it away faster than necessary.

The slight action didn't go unnoticed by Marc. A satisfied smile tilted one side of his mouth, and the laugh lines creased around his twinkling eyes. He watched her settle herself next to Paige on the middle seat as he gave the boat one last thrust and jumped into the front before his feet got wet. He carefully maneuvered between them to get to the back of the boat to man the motor. As he took the back seat, Samantha slipped up to the narrow seat in the front of the boat. He assumed it was to keep distance between them, but it suited him just fine because now she had to face him. It would be harder for her to ignore him when she was looking directly at him.

The first time he caught her eye he gave her a sexy wink and watched as the blush returned. A fierce glare was his answer, and she concentrated on Paige as he started the fifteen-horse Mercury motor, and headed out to the fishing hole familiar to both Marc and Samantha.

Quiet had settled over the water as they sat watching their bobbers in silence. The sun was low, and the birds in the nearby woods had settled down to a contented twittering. Two loons on opposite sides of the lake were communicating in their distinctive, haunting cry.

Several hefty crappies were already on the stringer, but the fisherman, woman, and child were patiently waiting for more to bite. There was a lull in both fishing activity and conversation. Paige was finally winding down after the excitement of landing her fish, with considerable help from both Marc and her mother. Her little arms were crossed on the side of the boat with her chin resting on them; the fishing rod tucked tightly between her legs so she wouldn't lose it over the edge. She had a hard time keeping her eyes open and every once in awhile her head would bob until finally she gave in, turned her cheek sideways, and fell asleep.

Marc noticed the sweet, sad smile that crossed Samantha's face as she watched her daughter.

"What are you thinking right now, Sam?" he murmured low so as not to wake the sleeping child. He was leaning back against the side of the boat with his long legs stretched out. His questioning eyes were on her, but his face was relaxed as he studied her intently.

The sad expression stayed as Samantha slid her gaze to the shoreline. "How times change I guess. How circumstances change us, who we are, what our future holds. Mostly how our dreams can fade into nightmares and what a struggle it is to try and climb back into the dream so you can wake up happy."

"Are you ever going to trust me enough to let me know why you carry those shadows in your eyes. I think it goes way beyond Rocky dying. What was your life like before he died? You seemed to have dropped off the face of the earth after you met him. Even your parents didn't see you much." He gathered his legs and leaned forward on his knees as he searched her eyes for an answer.

Samantha's glance darted to her sleeping child, not wanting her to hear this conversation. Paige's slight snore assured her she was sound asleep. "He didn't want me to have friends," she admitted. "He hated it when I came up to visit my folks and finally I just quit coming because it wasn't worth the hassle." She glanced again at her daughter. "He didn't even want kids because he didn't want any competition for my time. He was so angry when I got pregnant he threatened to leave." Her voice lowered to a whisper, "I wish he had."

Marc shifted his feet to rise, but stopped as she held up her hand. "Don't!" she said, tears threatening. "I can't handle it when anyone's nice to me. Don't feel sorry for me. I have to stay in control. If I let myself, I would be crying all of the time. Just give me a minute."

She turned away and Marc could see her drawing in deep breaths. He had never felt so helpless in his life. He wrapped up his line, then Paige's. Sam took it as a cue and pulled in her own line. Paige woke as he started the motor and Samantha moved to her side. Putting her arm around her daughter, she cuddled her close as they headed back to the resort.

The coolness of impending evening gave the air a chill, but it wasn't just the brisk atmosphere that engulfed them. A pall had settled over their fun-filled afternoon, but Marc had learned a lot more about what contributed to Samantha's shadowed gaze. He now realized why she was fighting so hard to keep him at arm's length, and knew he would have to be very careful to assure her he would never put his needs above hers.

All sorts of images and scenarios flashed through his mind as he maneuvered the watercraft back to the dock. Just what had Samantha been going through while he glibly went on with his life, having fun and doing whatever his heart desired. Meaningless relationships had come and gone. He had put in his time and did an excellent job at his work, but his heart hadn't been in any of it.

What would it have been like to live the life Samantha had just given him a glimpse of? Just from the little bit she had revealed, he deduced it was only a small portion of the problem. Knowing her, she had sugar coated it enough to hide the more gritty details.

What about Paige? Had she been too small to know what was going on, or were her memories bad enough to cause the problems she was experiencing now? Was it her father's death that was giving her nightmares, or was it his life?

Sitting behind Samantha and Paige, he watched as Sam laid her cheek on her daughter's messy curls. The colors were different but the unruly curls escaping from ponytails were the same. Sam's lighter hair was a contrast to Paige's dark brown, almost black tresses. Even though their backs were to him, he knew their eyes were almost identical, deep dark brown with long dark lashes and with a similar sadness behind the surface. Only when he could get them to laugh and forget their problems, could he observe the lighthearted humor beneath. He swore to himself he would find a way to bring that radiance forth, permanently.

Instead of beaching the boat, he carefully edged it up to the dock and grabbed a pole to hold it steady until he could get the rope out to tie it. Samantha quickly took the tie rope hooked on the bow of the boat and flipped it over another pole to secure it with a quick knot. The motions were smooth and quick, denoting that the docking had been done many times before. They knew what each was going to do before it needed to be done and accomplished the mooring without a word said.

It wasn't until he held out a hand to assist Sam from the boat to the dock that their eyes met. Her eyes implored him to let things go, to let her go. His eyes took on an obstinate firmness that, with a slight shake of his head, told her 'no way'. They had always been able to read each other's minds and anticipate what the other was going to say. It had only been heightened since their recent reunion.

With a sigh, Samantha hopped up on the deck and turned to catch Paige as Marc boosted her up so fast it made her giggle.

"Thanks for letting me go fishing with you, Pigeon. Tell you what. Because you let me join you, I'll clean the fish. Then some night you can come over to my place and we'll have a fish fry. Does that sound okay to you?"

"Sure Marc, where do you live? Do you live with your mom and dad, where we were the other day?" Paige questioned.

"Nope, I live in the old lodge further back from the lake." He turned to Samantha. "I'm living there while I'm remodeling it into a home. Since Mom and Dad built the new lodge and living quarters it's been sitting empty. It seemed a shame to let it go, so I'm slowly but surely fixing it up. It's livable, so we can have our fish fry there and I'll show you around." A satisfied smirk tipped one corner of his lips as he countered her fierce stare with a wink.

Why was he able to manipulate her so easily? Why did her heart give a leap whenever he gave that sexy smile? And how could she resist when he included Paige in his request? Between the two of them watching her, one pair of twinkling hazel eyes, the other dark and beseeching, she once again gave in.

With a resigned shake of her head she said, "It will have to be tomorrow evening after the guests have been taken care of. After that, I'll be tied up the rest of the week with resort work and payroll."

"Yes!" Paige's face broke into a grin as she pumped one arm and looked up at Marc, swinging her arm back for the expected high five.

She wasn't disappointed as he slapped her hand and grinned back at her. "Can you get your mom over by seven o'clock?" he asked.

"Sure," she said confidently, but one look at her mother's raised eyebrows made her stop, and with a guilty smile ask, "Is that okay, Mom?"

"Thank you for asking," Sam said wryly as she watched her animated daughter. She turned back to Marc, "Okay, we'll plan on being there by seven. Don't go to extra trouble. We're used to simple meals, and we'll have to leave right afterwards," she said pointedly. "Paige will have to get to bed."

"Point taken, ma'am," Marc chuckled. He reached down, lifted Paige and holding her in one arm, gave her a kiss on the cheek He then quickly leaned over and kissed Samantha on the cheek too. "G'night ladies, I've got some fish to clean," he said as he set Paige down and reached for the stringer of still-flopping pan fish. He relished the look of surprise and something else he saw in Sam's eyes as he turned away. Feeling good, he whistled a merry tune as he strolled down the shoreline towards home.

The warmth of his lips and the heady fragrance of a sexy male lingered with Sam as she watched his lean hips swagger down the beach. She envied his ability to be so carefree, so determined in the fact that happiness was only a heartbeat away. Would she ever be able to capture those feelings again? She had elusive glimpses of them while he was with her. It was when she was alone, frightened, and frustrated that she questioned her ability to ever let loose of her problems and be completely happy.

Samantha took extra time getting ready for their dinner at Marc's. For the first time in a long time, she added a light taupe eye shadow and brushed her already black eyelashes with an extra sheen of mascara. She abandoned the ponytail and brushed her long hair until it shone with golden highlights that framed her flawless, tanned face.

As Samantha and Paige approached the old lodge, Sam was having mixed feelings. She was excited about meeting Marc in his own surroundings, but apprehensive about how she would keep her own mounting sexual awareness of him concealed.

The sight of the lodge, nestled in huge old growth White Pines, brought back a flood of memories. The old, scarred logs were dark with age, but the roof had been redone with lighter cedar shingles. A clump of birch with their white bark gleaming in the golden sun was a contrast to the dark green pines that stood sentinel at the main entrance.

The lodge's main room had a tall peak with many windows facing the lake. She remembered the huge fieldstone fireplace surrounded by comfortable chairs and sofas where resort guests had once been welcome. That was before the lodge had been closed due to its lack of modern amenities. The modern building that was now the lodge and living quarters for Peggy and John, was beautiful, but she had a special feeling for the building she was now approaching.

After it was closed, this old historic building was where Jessie, Marc, and Sam, had spent a lot of their free time. They would play hide and seek in the empty rooms or occasionally have sleepovers, bringing sleeping bags and a ton of snacks. Halloween was always a special day because they would spend weeks setting it up as a haunted house and inviting their school friends for a fright-filled evening of screams, games and ghoulish fun.

She expected the memories of Marc as a kid to make her uncomfortable, surprisingly, they didn't. She was happy he was restoring the beautiful building that had meant so much to her.

As they drew closer, they could hear the loud music. Fifties Rock and Roll blared out of the open kitchen windows at the side of the lodge. She smiled back as Paige glanced up at her, a look of disbelief screwed up her little face. Still, both of them were bouncing to the heavy beat as they reached the door and knocked loudly. The distinct aroma of frying fish wafted out as he opened the door.

Marc found himself staring at Samantha. This was the first time he'd seen her with her hair down and the makeup subtly enhancing her beautiful eyes. With a deep breath he immediately caught himself. "Aha! My ladies have arrived!" Marc ushered them in. "Have a seat, I have to watch my cooking so I don't serve burnt offerings. Sam, there are drinks, fruit Jell-O, and a salad in the fridge. Mind grabbing them?"

As he turned back to the spattering pan she did as she was bidden. The table was already set haphazardly, and she finished adding the items from the refrigerator. His good mood and crazy jokes kept both Sam and Paige laughing as he served up the crispy, golden fillets.

The lighthearted banter kept up during the meal and continued as they started cleaning up the table. Samantha couldn't believe how good it felt to relax and have someone else take charge. How natural it felt to share in something as simple as household chores.

"Mom, why don't you know how to fry fish like Marc? That was really good!" Paige innocently questioned.

"Oh, oh!" Marc whispered. He and Sam were standing next to each other at the sink doing up the few dishes they had used. He slanted a glance at her and playfully bumped her shoulder with his. "I swear I didn't coach her to say that," he said, raising one soapy hand. Bubbles ran down his arm, threatening to dampen his rolled up sleeve.

"Sure you didn't! You've been conspiring against me every since you met her." Samantha was only half kidding as she jabbed a, not so gentle, elbow into his ribs. He hooked his elbow around her neck to hold her tight while his other soapy hand came out of the dishwater. He proceeded to dab the fluffy suds all over her face until she looked like Santa Claus. A giggling Paige jumped up and down with glee as she watched the adults' horseplay.

Samantha squealed and tried to pull away, but was engulfed in a two-armed bear hug while Marc took the opportunity to nuzzle into the soft nape behind her ear. Under the veil of her loose hair, he placed a wet kiss and drew his tongue along the shell of her ear. He felt her shudder, and only the presence of Paige stopped him from continuing his pursuit.

Not releasing her completely, he reached behind him for the dishtowel and smushed the cloth into her dripping face. He couldn't believe his eyes when he removed the towel and looked into her damp face. She was actually laughing. Her voluptuous lips were open, showing perfect white teeth, and a genuine smile lit up her face. A low throaty laugh consumed her and her eyes crinkled in glee.

Marc was mesmerized. He couldn't take his eyes from her face. He hadn't seen her look so happy since he had first noticed her on the dock. It reminded him of the old Sam. The one he grew up knowing and the one he had fallen in love with years ago. It gave him hope; hope that he could provide her with what she needed to overcome her fears and insecurities. With another quick hug and quick kiss on the forehead he released her.

Paige was tugging at Samantha's leg, aware that something had just happened but didn't know exactly what. Samantha had the same feeling. What had just happened? All she knew was that she suddenly felt free. Free to laugh, free to act silly, even free to give this big lug next to her a wink, as she bent to satisfy her daughter's concern and curiosity.

Samantha was impressed as Marc took them on the tour of the house. So far most of the renovations had been on the main floor, but the whole building had been cleaned and stripped of all the decaying wood and clutter. The great room still had the open beamed ceilings and walls made of knotty pine that gave her the feeling of being in the deep forest. It was clear that the rocks on the fireplace had been cleaned of accumulated soot but the split log mantel was the same one she remembered.

As Marc walked them back home, the sun was low on the horizon, just tipping the tops of the trees and coloring them a fiery amber. They were quiet as they strolled along with Paige in the middle and an adult holding each hand. He couldn't help wishing this could be permanent but knew it was too soon to push. Great progress had been made tonight with Sam opening up and having fun, and he didn't want to ruin it. So far he felt optimistic, but knew more time was needed for her to trust again. Even though he was impatient, he was resigned to keeping the relationship low key for the time being.

The summer was slipping by fast for Samantha. She was kept so busy she barely could keep track of time. What she did know was that tomorrow was the Fourth of July. Paige had been reminding her for days because she wanted to go to the parade in the small town of Shorecrest, and to the fireworks that night. She had been putting her off, but Marc had settled the question by coming over last night and inviting the both of them to go with him. She hadn't seen him since their fish fry and had to admit she had missed him. Paige had also been asking about him so she had happily accepted his invitation.

They were now standing in a throng of people watching the floats go by. The local fire trucks had just passed and sprayed the crowd, causing Paige to squeal as she tried to hide behind Marc. She was now standing a little distance from them, edging closer to the street so she could get more of the candy that the parade participants threw to eager kids.

Samantha stood close to Marc. He had an arm loosely around her with his hand cupping her opposite shoulder. His stance protected her from the surging crowd and at the same time was a subtle sign that she was with him. The action had already deterred a couple of over-eager playboys that had set eyes on her. She had been oblivious to their interest, but Marc had intercepted them with an icy stare that had them turning in their tracks.

Their attentions were now directed at an approaching float. The loud music and colorful streamers had everyone gawking to see what it was representing. Sam was standing on her tiptoes to see better when she heard a scream. She immediately turned to check on Paige. Frantically, she searched the area where her daughter had been standing and didn't see her anywhere.

"Marc!" she screamed, grasping his arm, "Paige is gone!" She tore through the crowd with Marc right behind her. Once again she heard a scream and ran towards it as she pushed and shoved her way through the oblivious crowd.

"There she is!" Marc lunged past her and she caught a glimpse of Paige, now standing alone and crying uncontrollably. By the time she got to them there was no one around, but she did see someone in a clown costume disappear into a light brown Chevrolet parked along the street. A few people had turned to watch but evidently thought it was some recalcitrant child and continued on to the parade route.

Marc had picked Paige up and was holding her tight; her arms held his neck in a death grip. His face was pale and his eyes shut. He opened them as he felt Samantha beside him and put an arm around her as she clutched her daughter. "Let's get out of here!" he choked. Samantha nodded in agreement and they carried the still sobbing little girl to Marc's pickup.

Chapter Five

Oh no! That was so close. Why did that kid have to scream? That mother doesn't deserve her. She should keep her away from crowds. She's mine! I want her!

I touched her though. Her skin is soft, so soft.

I have to think some more. I have to get closer. I have to plan. I have to make a better plan. There must be something somewhere that would work. I know I can do it. I just have to think about it.

She is so beautiful. Her skin is so soft, and I touched her hair, that beautiful hair.

Chapter Six

The rest of the afternoon was spent with both families together, trying to keep the incident low-key for Paige's sake. They had all congregated at the home of John and Peggy after a quick call from Marc had apprised them of the situation. The Hammonds had called George and Mary, explained what had happened, and invited them over. They had called the police and both families were sitting in the Hammonds' kitchen waiting for them by the time Marc and Samantha arrived with a still frightened Paige.

Shortly after Marc and Sam arrived, a squad car pulled into the yard and the whole incident was reported. Information was taken down, including the color and make of the car, but there could be no assurances because of a lack of evidence and no license plate number.

After they watched the squad leave, Marc pulled out a chair for Samantha, and Paige insisted on sitting on her lap. He pulled a chair close to both of them, and they thanked Peggy as she set steaming cups of coffee in front of them. A glass of chocolate milk with a plate of Oreo cookies was for Paige.

The adults kept the conversation light in front of Paige, but concern was etched in their faces. Paige herself was visibly shaken but anxious to talk about it. "The clown had a whole pail of candy." She explained. "He went like this," she beckoned with her hand as if urging someone forward. "I thought he was from the parade, so I went." Her voice started shaking as she continued, "When I stopped to look back for Mommy he grabbed my arm. I remembered what Mom had told me about strangers and I screamed and kicked him. Then he ran away."

"Do you remember anything about him? Like maybe, you've seen him, or heard the voice before?" Sam tried to keep her voice calm but was screaming inside. Her arms involuntarily gripped her daughter tighter.

Paige squirmed to loosen the hold and turned to look her in the face. "No, Mom! He had a mask and he didn't say anything. Like clowns, you know, they don't talk!" she said, her voice exasperated, like, grownups should know that.

"You're right, what was I thinking?" Samantha smiled down at her daughter. Deciding that was enough inquiry for now, she changed the subject. "Do you feel like going to the fireworks tonight? Marc said earlier we could all go out on his pontoon and watch them from the middle of the lake." She sent a questioning glance towards Marc and was surprised at the look on his face.

He had been sitting so still and quiet she hadn't noticed before, but now she saw how pale and drawn he looked. His eyes pleaded with her, but for once she couldn't read the message he was sending.

"John and Peggy would you mind if Mom and Dad stayed here a bit and you guys can watch Paige? I'd like to talk to Marc a minute, we'll be right back."

"Sampson, you know you're all welcome any time." John turned to the rest at the table. "What say we go into the living room where we'll be more comfortable.

"Sam, I don't think we can stay. One of the cabins has something wrong with the shower drain. I have to see to it," George apologized.

"And I have to run into town for supplies," Mary quickly added.

Sam just looked at her parents in disbelief. She couldn't think of a thing to say in response. Knowing how rundown the resort was, and that guests needed to come first, she knew her father was sincere in his apology. What she couldn't fathom was her mother's weak excuse. She herself had seen to it that all provisions had been stocked ahead of time. It was sometimes hard to find some items locally on a busy holiday weekend, so she always kept plenty in store.

Samantha felt Marc turn to look at her and felt his hand reach for hers under the table. She bit her bottom lip to keep from saying anything and nodded slowly at her mother. Mary flushed with embarrassment at the telling look in her daughter's eyes and quickly said her goodbyes as she scurried out the door.

John broke into the moment of silence and scooped Paige up in his arms. "Hey Paige, Jessie left one of her kids' DVDs here. Would you like to lay on the pillows and watch it?"

Paige nodded, her curly ponytail bobbing. "Can we still go to the fireworks?" she asked her mother with a child's persistence. She hadn't forgotten the question asked before.

"We'll talk about it." Her answer drew a resigned look from her daughter.

Paige took John's face in both hands and looked him in the eye as she said solemnly, "That usually means no!"

John laughed as he headed into the family room and ushered Peggy before him. He glanced back over his shoulder and gave Samantha a knowing look. A slow perusal of his son, now studying the tabletop, put worry back into his gentle eyes, but he was talking to Paige about the movie as he left the kitchen.

Once again Samantha was grateful for such a generous, understanding family. Although she knew her parents were worried, it was as though they wanted to separate themselves from the problem, and were glad to have someone else shoulder the burdens.

"Okay, Marc, let's go outside, I think we need to talk." It was unusual for her to take the initiative, but something in his eyes worried her. She led him to the secluded patio beneath the draping limbs of a weeping willow. There, she sat in the black, wrought iron, love seat and pulled him down next to her. His silence added to the fear that was still coiled as tight as a spring in her stomach. She could feel the tension in the way he held himself stiffly and by the faraway look in his eyes as he gazed unseeing over the lake.

"Marc." Samantha turned to face him. She took his hand in one of hers and tugged at his shirtsleeve with her other until he turned to her. "What's the matter, what are you thinking? You're scaring me."

"Forget it Sam, I think you should leave. Go someplace where you and Paige will be safe."

Her voice rose, "And where would that be? Why do you want me to leave all of a sudden? You've been telling me for the past month how you're glad I'm here. What's with the turnaround?" She dropped his hand and turned to face the lake. "You don't want to get involved in my problem with Paige. Right? That seems to be the way a lot of people feel right now. Maybe I should leave," her voice broke as she fought threatening tears. "You said you wanted to take care of us but I guess it looks like a bigger chore than you bargained for." She jumped up to leave. "Just forget it! I've been taking care of myself and Paige so far, I can do fine by myself!" She yelled at him, her voice hoarse with emotion.

Marc grabbed her arm as she whirled away. "Dammit! Sam! Don't you see? I failed to protect her! I promised and couldn't fulfill my promise. I was standing right there and didn't even see what was happening right under my nose! How good of a protector is that?" His face was contorted in self-derision. All of the soft, good humor was gone from his camouflage eyes. They were dark as a storm cloud and clouded with pain. "I didn't even think to wait and tell the authorities! I panicked and all I could think of was getting her out of there! Maybe they could have caught whoever it was."

Samantha's heart flipped as she looked down into his anguished face. She saw guilt on the somber face that was becoming so important to her. Deep grooves marred his brow. Now she knew why he had been so withdrawn since they had arrived home. He blamed himself for the near abduction. His feelings must have been mirroring her own, she was sure it was *her* negligence that had allowed the incident to happen.

She cupped his jaw and rubbed her thumb slowly over his cheek. "Marc, it wasn't your fault," she murmured, as she tipped his face up so she could study his eyes. "I was standing right there too. I've been going over in my head what I could have done, should have done. Short of putting her on a leash, I don't know what I could have done differently. I guess I was lulled into thinking her stories weren't true because nothing has happened lately. Now that we know differently, we'll have to keep her in sight all of the time."

Marc leaned his head into her hand as he pulled her onto his lap. He turned his mouth enough so he could place a warm kiss in the palm of her hand. Then he raised his hand to the back of her head and threaded his fingers through her loose hair as he pulled her forward to meet his lips. She moved her hand to cup the back of his head and opened her mouth to his.

A fusion of conflicting emotions ignited their passion the second their lips met. Their volatile feelings, heightened by the tremendous scare they had endured, exploded. Mouths meshed and tongues mated only to be released and captured again and again. Their breathing was labored and hands sought forbidden places when the sound of a boat approaching the resort brought them back to reality.

Samantha pulled away and took a deep breath. She looked into the expressive eyes that were now dark with passion. "I'd better go check on Paige," she whispered. Confusion furrowed her brow. She couldn't separate her rampant emotions. Guilt flooded back, erasing the fervent feelings that had heated her blood and clouded her mind. "What kind of a mother am I?" she questioned.

Although she directed the question to herself, Marc couldn't help but take the remark personally. He lifted her off his lap and stood, keeping hold of her arms as he looked into her eyes. "What you're really asking is, what kind of man am I, isn't it? You are really wondering how I can become so immersed in you that I can put aside what happened to Paige!"

"No, Marc! It isn't you, it's me, I'm her mother! I'm sorry, but I don't have room in my life for anyone else right now. I have to do this myself. I have to protect Paige, and I have to find out who's stalking her!" Her voice rose as she turned her back to him and started towards the house.

"Samantha!" Marc strode toward her, gripped her arms from behind and pulled her against him. He wrapped his arms around her and held her tight to prevent her from struggling loose. He buried his face in her hair and just held her but could not find the right words to reassure her. The fright that had him shaking was the fear of losing his role to protect, not only the little girl that was now a part of him, but this woman that he had loved for so many years.

"Marc," Sam's voice was quiet and resigned. Her hands gently caressed the arms that were crossed across her chest. She allowed herself to lean back against him for a brief moment, relishing the warmth and comfort of being held so safely. "I'm so sorry. There are things I have to do, problems I have to fix, and no matter what you say or what we feel, I have to try to correct them on my own."

Suddenly, Marc loosened his grip and turned her to face him. Controlled rage had infused his demeanor. He looked deep in her eyes and said, "Just remember, this isn't what I want!" He gripped her arms and pushed her back. "I can't keep being shoved aside!" He didn't trust himself to say more so turned on his heel. Not wanting to face his parents, he headed towards his own house.

Samantha watched him leave. Her whole chest hurt at his angry stride and stiff back. She felt as though any chance of a future relationship had just walked away on furious feet.

Visibly composing herself, she lifted her chin and squared her shoulders as she took a deep breath and strode towards the lodge to pick up Paige. She'd been through worse than this, she told herself, and she would survive. Fighting back tears she opened the door.

Peggy looked up from her knitting when Samantha walked in. From Sam's demeanor, and the look of devastation on her face, Peggy felt an ominous cloud envelope her. A quick look at John and Paige assured her that they were both sound asleep in front of the TV where dancing penguins happily danced in silence. She motioned Sam to follow her into the kitchen.

"Sam, what's wrong?" Peggy reached out to clasp Samantha's cold as ice and trembling hand.

"Peggy, I'm sorry but I have to take Paige. I have to find out what's going on, and, I have to do it myself."

"But, what about Marc? What is this going to do to him? Samantha, you must know how he feels about you and Paige."

"I don't feel right involving him in this. I have no idea what's going on here, and it isn't fair to any of you to upset your family too. Peggy, I really appreciate your friendship and willingness to help, but there's more going on than you know." Sam's voice was trembling and tears again threatened to fall. "I'll miss you more than you'll ever know. I have always felt so at home here."

Peggy started forward but Samantha anticipated the hug and turned away. She knew if she allowed the warmth and compassion she saw in Peggy's eyes to touch her, she wouldn't have the strength to follow her decision to leave.

Sam turned to the other room and almost lost it when she saw her daughter cuddled safely in John's arms. Both of them were sleeping safely; her baby being protected by a gentle giant.

John woke up as she tried to extricate Paige from his arms. "Hey Sampson, where's Marc?" His voice was still rough from his nap.

"He went home," she whispered, trying to pick Paige up without waking her.

"Home? I thought you guys were going to the fireworks?" At the stricken look on her face, he glanced up at Peggy who was solemnly shaking her head and gesturing for him to be quiet. Slowly, he got to his feet and helped Sam get Paige into her arms.

As she made her way out of their lodge with her limp daughter in her arms, she turned at the door and mouthed, "I'm sorry." Her face crumpled, and she couldn't hold back the sob that escaped as she hitched the little girl higher and slowly walked away, her face buried in the little girl's hair.

Leaving three of her favorite people was the hardest thing she had ever done. It was even harder than when Rocky had died. The confusion and pain she had witnessed in their expressions, stayed with her for a long time.

A few days after the frightening incident, Samantha once again began to get her footing. The pain was a little less and she just didn't have the option of sitting around feeling sorry for herself. Paige was the one area that she was vigilant about, and she never let her guard down. Her daughter never left her side unless she was with her grandparents.

Sophie, one of the cleaning women had called in this morning and reported she had fallen and sprained her ankle so couldn't come to work. At her suggestion, Sam had agreed to hire her niece, who was on summer break from college, to fill in until Sophie could come back.

Brenda had just arrived and Sam immediately had second thoughts. Who would actually show up for a housekeeping job dressed like that? She wore skin tight, white jeans with a red, low, scoop neck tee shirt, that didn't quite cover the cleavage. Long, bleached blonde hair that swirled around her face and bright red fingernails, long enough to scratch her back from any position completed the package.

Samantha just shook her head and decided she wasn't giving this girl any breaks. If she didn't know any better now, she would learn quickly enough. Sam took her to the cabin that was being cleaned, showed her what to do, and left. She wasn't in any mood to show mercy this morning.

 Her mother had been out late last night, and Sam knew she had been gambling again. Samantha had been on her way to have a talk with her when she heard about Sophie. Now she couldn't and wouldn't put it off any longer.

Even the warmth of the morning sun and the beautiful surroundings couldn't detract her from her next mission. She embraced the turmoil within that Brenda had fueled. Maybe the anger she was feeling would toughen her up enough for the confrontation she knew lay ahead.

"Mom!" She called when she got back to the lodge. "Where are you?"

"Back here with Paige where you told me to be. Where did you think I could go with her along?" Mary answered in a petulant voice that set Sam's teeth on edge.

"Paige, would you go up to your room for awhile? I need to talk to Grandma." Sam ignored the fierce look Mary shot at her. "Okay, Mom," she started, as soon as Paige had reluctantly left the room. "I don't know where you got the money and I'm not even going to ask. I do know where you went and that you lied to me and Dad." The firmness in her voice belied the queasy feeling she had in her stomach from confronting her mother.

Sam was surprised when the belligerence left her mother's face. All of a sudden she was looking at a trampled woman. Mary's shoulders slumped and she covered her face rather than look at her. Sam was further surprised when her mother started to cry. Suddenly, she realized how serious the problem was; so serious that she now knew for sure that it was something her mother couldn't conquer on her own.

"Mom, it's okay. If you will just let me, we can work on this together. I've already looked into several places that you could go for help. I was just waiting for you to realize you have a problem and admit it. That's the first step to recovery. You have to want to quit gambling or it is useless." Samantha knelt by her mother's chair and grasped her clenched hands.

"Sam, I'm so embarrassed." Mary's voice cracked as she tried to control her crying. She reached for a tissue and blew her nose before she looked up and met her daughter's gaze. "I don't know how I got hooked. For years it was just fun then it became an obsession. I just had to go. There's nothing like the rush I feel when I'm gambling. Then when I have to stop it hits me. What I've done again and how much I've lost. I get so depressed." She reached out and laid her hand on Sam's arm. "Then I get crabby and defensive. I know it's been hard on you and George. It's just so hard to admit I've caused so much trouble for the resort, and for all of you."

"We can all work together on this, Mom. We want to help. It's killing Dad the way you treat him. He isn't the villain. He's worried about you and about trying to keep the resort afloat. Don't treat him like he did something wrong by confronting you." Samantha stood as she continued, "And don't try to continue making me feel guilty either. You know we didn't have any other choice."

As hard as it was, Sam stood firm and unyielding as her mother, once again, started to sob. She had tried trusting her and now she knew she had to get more involved. Tomorrow they were going to a counselor that was trained in the compulsive disorder that had control of her mother's life.

Several times during the next couple of weeks, Samantha had to summon the inner strength it took to stay firm with the decision to push her mother into following through with the plans for treatment of her illness.

Although Grand Rapids would have been closer, her mother's fear of running into someone she knew made her adamantly dismiss that idea. They set up meetings in Duluth, and as much as Sam felt she should go with her, she knew her first priority was her daughter. Paige was already getting impatient with never being allowed to run free and with always having an adult within sight.

"Dad, I assure you it will be better if you go with her. If you listen and participate, maybe it will help you to understand. I'm struggling with the concept of anyone being so dependent on the gambling fever and I know you are too."

"Yes, Sam, but that will mean you will be here alone at the resort. Not only will you have to keep extra watch over Paige, you will have the resort to run." It was obvious her dad was torn between his responsibilities, but she was adamant about him being the one to accompany her mother to the meetings.

"I can manage the afternoons you'll be gone. You will both be here for the weekends and that's the hectic time." Sam knew she was stretched to the limit already, but not having to worry about her mother would be one burden she could lay down if her dad would step up to the plate on this one.

She was relieved when he finally agreed, and the necessary arrangements and schedules were worked out.

Chapter Seven

"Damn! Not again!" As much as she hated herself for it, she couldn't help watching down the shoreline to see if she could catch a glimpse of Marc. Just knowing he was close and catching sight of him now and then was enough to send conflicting emotions surging through her. The fact that he took her at her word and would not initiate any contact was a relief and a torture. Just the thought of him had her remembering their embraces, and the happiness he could bring, with just the teasing grin and a sparkle in his eye. Happiness she had given up and sorely missed.

Right now, however, a slow burn crept up her collar as she recognized the long blonde hair of Brenda, as she all but crawled over him while he worked on one of the boats. This wasn't the first time she had noticed her new employee over there, nor was there any question in her mind why Brenda decided to wander over that way when her shift was over.

Samantha knew it was unreasonable for her to have these feelings. Hadn't she been the one to insist she couldn't continue with the relationship? She had to admit to herself that she was jealous. Just pure green-eyed jealousy was eating at her every time she saw Brenda over at the neighboring resort.

It didn't help any that, whenever Marc saw her watching, he would give her an unemotional stare and then turn back, supposedly interested in what Brenda was saying. Just now, Sam watched the blonde reach up to brush a lock of hair back off his forehead and gritted her teeth in frustration. Deciding it was too painful to watch, she threw the rake she was using to clean debris off the beach into her wheelbarrow, and stomped back towards the garage.

Out of the corner of his eye, Marc watched Samantha flounce off and a satisfied smirk lifted the corner of his mouth. Even though Brenda was getting on his nerves, maybe being seen with her would shake Sam enough so she would start thinking about what they had been building together. He sensed that Brenda was just whiling away her time flirting with him anyway. She was the type who had to have male attention, and for the summer he was the closest target.

It was several days later that he began to get the hint he was playing the part too realistically when his mother cornered him.

"What on earth are you doing with that bimbo? I swear if you let her hang around here any longer I'm going to have a few words with her. They won't be words that are easy on the ears either. She has to be the dumbest creature on earth, and if I see her touch my husband one more time, she's going to get more than words."

The longer Peggy talked, the more steamed she got; her face turned so red it almost matched the prominent freckles that were her trademark.

"Relax, Mom. She'll only be around a little longer. I assure you. I know she is as annoying as hell, but she's actually part of a plan I've just devised."

"Marcus! What are you thinking? If this has to do with Sam, I can't emphasize enough that you are treading in very dangerous waters. What if it backfires on you? I can only assume you are talking about making her jealous. What if she decides you have moved on and she will do the same?"

"Trust me, Mom. Trust me." Marc's grin spread across his face and crinkled his eyes. He looped an arm around his mom's shoulders and gave her a quick hug. "I gave her some time, let her think I'd given up, but there is no way in hell I'm letting her off this easy. Mom, you don't know what we have together and it isn't just me. I can tell she's interested, just fighting it tooth and nail."

"Son, you have to respect the fact that she has problems other than you. Although I must admit you *are* enough problem for the poor woman even if she didn't have any others. I think you should give her some time and space. I'm confident she will work her way through things. Just give her some time."

"Nope, I know her well enough to know she will never admit her feelings, nor will she admit she can't do everything herself. She needs a little nudge now and then or she will crawl back into her shell and throw up some more barriers. In fact, I feel another nudge coming on right now." He looked down the beach to see the now familiar bleached blonde heading towards them. It was late afternoon and she had evidently finished work.

"Crap! I'm getting out of here before she sees me! You just remember what I've said. These are people's feelings you're messing with. Including mine. Don't make me hurt you!" Peggy waggled her finger under his nose and heard his laugh as she turned on her heel and scurried inside.

"Hey Marc, what'cha doin' tonight?"

Brenda snuggled up so close to Marc's chest he almost took a step backward until he remembered his plan. "I don't have plans, did you have something in mind?"

"I just heard about the dance they're having at the Legion and thought maybe you and I could go together."

As Brenda issued the invitation she was running her fingers up and down his chest, batting mascara-thick eyelashes that reminded him of silver-screened vamps in classic movies. He almost burst out laughing at her before he caught himself. "You know what? I've a bit more to do around here, but why don't you go on ahead, and when I get done, I'll come on down, maybe run into you later." There was no way he was picking her up and then being expected to take her home. Even he wasn't that stupid.

Her disappointment was obvious in her pout, but she evidently figured that was all she could expect, so capitulated and leaned in to leave a red kiss on his cheek. She lingered as she did so, hoping he would follow up on the invitation. When he didn't respond she backed off with a flirtatious, "See you later then," and swayed off with an exaggerated swing of the hips.

"Oh, my God!" Marc thought, "This better be worth it!" That type of woman was one of the reasons he was still a bachelor. Another reason was the dormant wisp of a dream that had, until lately, given him the hope of it blossoming into fruition.

"Why, oh why, did I let myself get talked into this?" Samantha muttered as she wove through the crowd with a tray of Sloppy Joe hamburgers and fries held high to dodge some of the rowdy patrons at the dance. The fundraiser was for a local child that had been injured in a car accident, and when one of the Legion members had asked if she would help, she just couldn't say no. Her last excuse was shattered when her parents said they would be happy to watch Paige.

She took a second to think about the difference in both her mom and dad since the counseling had started. It had been a long time since she had seen the camaraderie between them that they now demonstrated. A sigh of relief left her as she delivered the lunch and headed toward the kitchen.

The dancing had started again, and she had to scoot around the revelers by staying close to the booths located on the outside walls. As she approached the last booth, she heard a familiar voice exclaim, "Oh, oh, here comes The Cougar, better hide, Marc!"

Samantha swung her head around and encountered the smirk on Brenda's face as she deliberately laid her hand on Marc's shoulder and leaned into him. The challenge was evident in the bold look she threw Sam.

A cold chill ran down Samantha's spine, and even though she told herself to keep walking, she stopped and her gaze swung to encounter Marc's. The moment lasted long enough for everyone to notice, and the other people in the booth became quiet as they felt the electricity crackle around them.

Sam finally raised one eyebrow and murmured, "Cougar?" That was the only word that was spoken as she broke eye contact and turned away. She kept her back as stiff as a broomstick as she made her way back to the kitchen.

She immediately made her excuses and said she had to leave. There was no way she could face Marc while he sat there with that cat. She made a mental note to call Sophie, and if she couldn't come back yet, she would advertise for another housekeeper, something she kicked herself for not doing after the first day of *Miss Centerfold*.

She was shaking by the time she entered her car, and curled her arms around the steering wheel as she leaned her head on them. She took a shuddering breath, desperately trying to keep from either bawling or screaming.

"Shit!" Marc gritted his teeth as he placed his elbows on the table. He dropped his forehead onto the heels of his hands; his fingers threaded through, and gripped his hair.

When he raised his head, he looked directly at Brenda who was watching him with a bewildered look. "You are fired! If you come anywhere near our resorts, I swear I will personally kick your ass!"

He shoved himself up, and with one last disgusted look, turned his back, and trotted toward the door. He missed the daggers Brenda shot at him through squinted eyes. If looks could kill he would have dropped dead in his tracks.

He stopped when he got to the parking lot and scanned for a familiar vehicle. The lot was overflowing onto the nearby streets so it took him several minutes before he located the dusty sedan with her resort logo on the door, parked on the grass.

The wind had picked up and lightening flickered in the western sky. Thunder rumbled off in the distance, and the acrid, earthy smell of impending rain assailed the senses.

Grateful that she hadn't left yet, he maneuvered so he could approach from behind the car. There was no doubt in his mind that if she saw him coming she would take off like a rabbit.

Guilt washed over him as he noticed her head down on her arms; the only movement was the heaving breaths she was taking.

The window was open so he quickly reached behind her and removed the keys from the ignition. "We've got to talk!" He said, as she jerked upright and reached for the keys in his hand.

"Talk!" She shrieked, "Talk!" An uncontrollable anger replaced the humiliation and depression that had sent her slinking out of the club like a whipped puppy. "Get your ass back in to that kitty cat. This *Cougar* can take care of herself! Now give me my damn keys!"

As she reached for the keys, Marc pulled them back out of her reach. "Fine! I'll find another ride home." She flipped up the armrest and started to clamber over the console to reach the opposite door. She almost made it before a firm hand clamped around her wrist. Marc had climbed in far enough to snag her before she could escape out the other side.

"Christ, Sam! Stop it!" You're going to break something," Marc's voice raised in exasperation as she tried to wrest her arm free.

"Listen to me for just a minute. I'm not with her, Sam. We met here. And for your information, you better get a new worker because I just fired her for you." He pulled her back into the car and slipped into the driver's seat without loosening his grip. "Do me a favor, Samantha. I'll let you go if you can explain to me why you are so upset."

Her angry gaze flashed up to meet his somber stare, neither blinked for a long, silent moment. She broke the connection first, as she sat back and switched her focus to the first raindrops splashing on the windshield.

"I think you know why I'm upset but I'm not ready to go there right now. I think I've helped my mother get on the right track now, but I still have Paige to worry about." She swung her head to face him. "You're right. I'm jealous, and I have no right to be."

Marc cupped her face in his hand and tipped her chin so his lips could capture hers with a gentle caress. "You could have every right if you should ever decide to let it happen. My mother was right, it was a stupid idea to make you jealous and I apologize."

"You deliberately planned this? You are a real shit-head do you know that? And Peggy knew? Well, good for her for taking my side, I'll have to thank her and give my condolences on having given birth to a shit-head!" Anger was still evident in her voice, but was now it was tempered with the realization that he still cared enough to ignore her protests.

A brilliant flash of lightening was followed immediately by a crack of thunder that shook the earth and had her snatching her keys out of his hand. "Now get out of this weather before you get struck by lightening, I have to go check on Paige and Mom and Dad."

"Not so fast!" Marc whispered as he maneuvered in the tight space to turn toward her. One hand slipped to her waist the other clasped her nape and slowly drew her forward. Their eyes met and held as their mouths softened in anticipation.

Her eyes closed at the first feather-like touch of his lips and warmth coursed through her as she sank into his embrace. His fingers tugged the ponytail band from her hair and he threaded his fingers through the silken tresses to clasp her head more tightly. His mouth now consumed hers with deepening kisses. A soft moan nearly drove him over the edge as his hand slid under her shirt and moved up to cover her breast.

"Uh! Uh!" She managed to murmur against his lips. "I said I have to get home. This storm is getting worse."

"There's a storm raging in me worse than what's outside of this car. You could put the fire out if you wanted to." He nuzzled against her ear as he whispered the words.

Reluctantly, he slowly set her back with another gentle peck on her swollen lips and stepped out of the car.

He stood in the pouring rain and watched as she exited the parking lot. It wasn't until she was out of sight that he shivered from the cold rain and realized what an idiot he must look like, standing out in a tempest that rivaled the turbulence within his chest.

Samantha kept an eye on him as she turned out of the parking lot and entered the street. Why couldn't she just accept the fact that she was crazy over that handsome brute and stop worrying about the consequences? What was it that made her think life had to be perfect for her family before she allowed herself the privilege of happiness for herself? No answers came to mind, so she gave herself a mental shake and concentrated on the wet and windy drive home.

Chapter Eight

Sam was wound up as tight as a clock spring when she finally drove up the driveway to the lodge. Torrential rain and flying branches made the drive take twice as long as it usually did. She suspected, but didn't know for sure, that the dim headlights in her rear view mirror were Marc's because they continued on after she turned off into the driveway of the resort. It made her feel safe and even more confused that he would continue to watch over her even after she had put him off again.

She arrived at her door after a mad dash through the whirling, pelting rain and was surprised that she found it unlocked. She shrugged it off; deciding her parents had left it open for her, and thankful that she didn't have to take time to dig her keys out while standing in the deluge.

After shedding her wet jacket and depositing her soggy sneakers on the mat by the door, she took a deep breath. Emotions bombarded her, and she knew she couldn't get to sleep even if she tried. She filled the teakettle and turned the stove on under the burner. "Chamomile," she said to herself, "Let's see if it really does what they say about relaxing you."

A half hour later she still couldn't definitively say whether it did or not, but she was feeling more tired. Knowing she had another busy day ahead of her, she decided to turn in and headed up the stairs. Half way up, a strange feeling came over her. Slowing, she proceeded up the stairs cautiously.

She quietly opened the door to Paige's room and peeked in. There was only the light from the hallway, which was strange because Paige always insisted that a night-light be left on. She could see a bunched up bedspread and walked in. When she didn't see the curly black hair, she jerked the covers back.

"Paige!" The scream echoed back through the hallway. Samantha's heart almost stopped beating before it started pounding so hard her chest ached.

She flew down the hall so fast she didn't even remember it, and jerked her parent's door open. "Paige is gone!" she shrieked.

"Samantha, be quiet!" Mary whispered. "Paige is in here with us."

"What's the matter?" George mumbled as he sat up in bed and rubbed his hand over his face.

"Sam thought Paige was missing, go back to sleep." Mary pushed back the covers as she swung her legs over the bed.

Sam saw Paige tucked in between her grandparents on the king sized bed. Her relief was so intense she held onto the doorjamb and sunk to the carpet. An uncontrolled trembling shook her body and had Mary rushing to her side.

"Samantha! What's the matter?" Mary whispered, as she knelt by her daughter and held her tight until the shaking subsided. "Come on Samantha, let's go downstairs. You can't go on like this. You're driving yourself too hard, worrying too much. Come now, get up and come with me." She stood and gently pulled Sam up with her. Quietly closing the bedroom door, she urged her daughter towards the stairs.

Arm in arm they descended the stairs but this time it was Mary's strength that Samantha depended on. Consciously or unconsciously, roles were reversed, at least for the moment.

Samantha sunk into the captain chair and rested her elbows on the table, her hands crossed across her forehead, as she leaned into them. As the terror began to diminish she took a deep cleansing breath. "What on earth happened? Why was Paige in your room?" she asked.

Mary set a steaming cup of microwaved milk in front of Samantha and sat down across from her. Her cure for any late night trauma was hot milk. Although it wasn't Sam's favorite, she didn't argue and sipped dutifully.

"I don't know, Sam, I guess it was the storm that woke her up. She screamed and when I went to see what the problem was she told me she had seen a ghost. She said it was standing at the foot of her bed, but I thought it was probably just the flashing of the lightening and the thunder that woke her."

"Mom, when I came home the door was unlocked. Could someone have gotten in? Could she have really seen someone?"

"I don't think so, Sam. We did leave the door open for you, but when the storm started, and Paige got frightened, George came down and locked it. Are you sure it was unlocked?"

"I am certain it was unlocked."

"Oh my God!" Mother and daughter issued the same exclamation as their eyes met in horror.

"Someone was in the house! They were probably right here when George came down to lock up!" Mary's voice shook at the enormity of what must have happened. "They must have unlocked the door and let themselves out after we took Paige into our room."

"I didn't see any sign when I came in. You would think there would have been wet tracks or something."

"But Sam, it wasn't raining yet. The thunder and lightning were crashing before the rain ever started. We were sure that was what wakened Paige and that the flashing of the lightening was what she must have seen."

"Should we call the police? What would we tell them? We don't know anything for sure." Samantha stood and began pacing the floor. "We can't be positive anyone was here. They would question Paige, again! I'm sure whoever was here didn't leave any fingerprints. If I were going to break into someone's house, I know I would be careful to wear gloves. Any footprints outside would be long gone with that downpour out there."

"Why don't we wait until morning? You're exhausted and so am I. Let's try to get some sleep and maybe something will come to us. There is nothing the police would do tonight anyway. Come with me while I double check to make sure the house is empty and the doors and windows are locked.

"Should we wake Dad up to help?"

"No, let's not bother him. I doubt there is anyone here as long as the door was unlocked. I'll just feel better with a quick look around."

After a thorough examination of the house, they returned to the kitchen. Mary stood before her daughter and took her in her arms. "I'm sorry Sam, sorry for what I've put you through. Sorry for adding to your worries, sorry I haven't been there, or understood just what a burden you've been under. I'll do better from now on. We'll work this out together, I promise." Tears were in her eyes as she stepped back and looked into her daughter's eyes. She gripped her shoulders and gave a little shake. "I love you."

"I love you too, Mom." The words between them seemed awkward; neither had said them to each other often enough, but tonight they were sincere. Tonight they both, individually, made a vow to correct the mistakes of the past and work towards a better, closer relationship.

Sam pushed the chairs back in around the table, "You go on up Mom. I have a phone call to make."

"A phone call? It's pretty late to be calling anyone. Are you sure it can't wait until morning?"

"I'm sure, Mom. I have a feeling he'll be awake."

"He?"

"Okay Mom, I'm calling Marc." Sam said, resigned to the fact that it was time to get everything out in the open. "He was at the Legion tonight and things happened that sort of brought things to a head. We ended up talking, and I'm beginning to think I might have been wrong to deny this thing between us."

Samantha leaned against the counter top and raked her fingers through her hair; pulling it back and massaging her scalp as the loose strands filtered through her fingers. "I really thought it was best to not see him and just concentrate on Paige. It isn't really working and I don't know how it happened, but he really got under my skin. Even Paige keeps bugging me about him. She really misses him too.

"Good!" Mary surprised Sam with the exclamation. " I'm glad you're finally admitting it. I think you worry too much about the age difference. It's so obvious he's crazy about you and Paige. It's also obvious that you can never keep your eyes off him." She covered a yawn with her hand. "Now I'm going back to bed and I'll see you in the morning. Good luck with your phone call," she said with a sly grin.

With another quick hug for her daughter, she slowly climbed the stairs again, exhaustion evident in her slow steps. Half way up she turned and softly said, "He isn't Rocky, Sam. Don't blame him just because he's a man. Rocky was wrong for you from the beginning and I'm just sorry for the pain he put you through. Don't let it ruin the rest of your life. You have to learn to trust again."

Marc was sitting in the dark before the large windows, watching the waning storm diminish in strength. Only the occasional flicker of lightning across the lake illuminated the night sky. The branches had ceased thrashing against side of the house and the only sound was the final, soft dripping off the trees and his pounding heartbeat.

The condensation from the cold Coors in his hand was making a wet ring where it rested on his denim-clad thigh. A finger slowly circled the rim.

Thoughts were racing through his mind of his conversation with Samantha, and thoughts of the softness of her lips. He was also feeling the frustration of the complex relationship and finally, of hope. Hope that she wouldn't again disappear into her shell or find another excuse that would keep them apart.

His musings were interrupted by the shrill ringing of the telephone that caused him to jerk and spill the cold contents of the can into his lap. "Damn! This better be good," he muttered as he wiped ineffectually at the wet stain. "Hello!" He was sure he sounded crabby, but at this time of night he really didn't care. It was probably a wrong number anyway - who would be calling him this time of the night, or morning by now?

"Did I wake you up? Should I call back in the morning?"

"Sam! No, I just spilled beer in my lap. What's wrong? What happened?"

"Does something have to happen for me to call you?"

"Well, you do realize that it's past midnight and this is the first time you've ever called don't you?"

Her silence was a telling moment that made him even more curious. When she finally answered, it was with a soft, wistful voice. "I know, I just thought it was time. I miss you. I miss the fun times we had and I just wanted to tell you before I go to bed."

"Wow. Sam, I'm coming over," he murmured.

"No, Marc, not now, I'm really tired. Mom and I have been up and I really have to try to sleep. It's not going to be easy after what happened tonight, but I've got a big day tomorrow. I just wanted to talk to you a minute. You make me feel safe."

"Safe? Sam what happened now? Is Paige okay?" Fear coursed through Marc as a premonition engulfed him. "Something did happen. What? What happened tonight?"

It took only a few minutes for Samantha to fill him in, but that was long enough for Marc to feel his anger rise. How dare someone invade her privacy like that? What motive would anyone have for harming Paige? More questions assailed his mind, questions he had no answers for. Although he wanted to do something, anything, he knew it should wait for morning.

"Sam, you go to bed now. Call me when you wake up and I'm coming over first thing. Try to get some sleep, and Sam, you don't know how happy you've made me with this phone call." His voice lowered, "Just don't have a change of heart before morning. Stick with the feelings you're having right now. I know things will be better from now on. We'll work the problems out, *together!*"

"Goodnight, Marc. Even though I'm still worried about Paige, I feel as though a weight lifted from me when I made the decision to call you. See you in the morning."

Chapter Nine

Another mess up! When I saw her mother at the Legion, I was sure I could get to her this time. I have to wait until she is far away from the family, that's for certain. She has lungs like an opera singer. The next time I'll make sure no one can hear her. There must be some way to keep her quiet. I know one way!

She is so beautiful, even in the flash of lightening strikes! Such a pretty little girl! I'm sure lucky that the old man didn't check the pantry when he locked the doors. That was too close. It has to be the next time, my chances are running out. I have to think, it's getting harder to concentrate. I have to think! I need to have that beautiful child!

Chapter Ten

The next morning Marc arrived five minutes after Sam called him. She was dressed in shorts and a tee shirt, but by the disheveled hair and dark rings under her eyes, apparently hadn't gotten much sleep. She stood as he entered and sank into his outstretched arms. Neither said a word as he buried his face in her neck, each relishing the moment. She felt wanted and protected in his warm embrace. He was wishing they could stay that way forever.

But the world invaded their space, and they slowly separated as her parents and Paige descended the stairs. He stole a quick kiss before letting her go, but one arm still held her close. Paige was bouncing down the steps still in her pajamas, chattering to her Grandpa about the ghost she saw the night before. Mary's glance caught Samantha's gaze, and a silent message transferred itself from one to another.

"Marc!" Paige squealed as she saw their visitor. She flew off the bottom step and he let Sam go to catch the whirling dervish that caught him around the knees. He bent to catch her and threw her up in the air before catching her in a bear hug.

Tears came to his eyes as she wrapped her arms around his neck and placed a smacking kiss on his cheek. "I missed you," she whispered in his ear, chubby arms in a strangle hold as she squeezed tight.

"I missed you too, Pigeon. I missed you too!" he said, his eyes locking with Sam's through the dark curls that lay against his cheek. He was surprised to see tears in her eyes too, and a fist pressed against her lips to suppress a sob. He released one arm that was holding Paige and wrapped it around Sam's neck pulling her in to complete the trio.

George and Mary just stood and watched in silence, their hands automatically reaching for each other. This seemed so right, seeing Sam and Paige being held so tenderly. The tensions that had been building since their daughter and granddaughter had returned were eased. Hopefully, they would be protected now. Hopefully, there would be no more sinister sightings, but the doubts still lingered. Who had been in their house last night?

The sheriff's deputy had just left. Once again the story had been told with the focus centered on Paige. A preliminary search had been completed with nothing found, just as Sam had predicted.

They were seated around the table and bright sunshine illuminated the kitchen while they had a minimal breakfast. Paige was busy naming the alphabet as she chased the floating letters around the milk in her bowl. The adults were having toast with strawberry jam as no one felt up to a large breakfast. Even the cheery brightness of the day couldn't chase the somber thoughts each was harboring.

"I've got an idea." Marc decided it was time to break the mood. "Jessie is coming with the kids this morning. Sam, why don't you and Paige come over to Dad and Mom's and visit them. They have a new puppy they're bringing to show us. I bet Paige would like to play with it and her crew." His questioning glance incorporated George and Mary, silently asking their permission.

"Sure, that sounds like a good idea. Sunday is a quiet day around here and the guests are all settled in by now," George said, and Mary nodded her agreement.

"Go ahead Sam, I think it would be good for both you and Paige to have a distraction right now." Mary glanced towards Paige, who was tipping her bowl to slurp the last of the sugary milk.

"That's settled then. I'll give you awhile to get dressed and will be back to get you in an hour or so." Marc pushed himself up from the table and Sam rose to stand next to him.

"You don't have to come get us. We can walk along the beach, can't we Paige?"

"Okay, Mom. Can we look for more agates?" Paige wiped her milky mouth with the sleeve of her pajamas.

"I'm coming to pick you up!" Marc's voice was firm and brooked no argument.

Samantha gave him a sideways look, but didn't respond, as she would have any other day. Maybe he was right. She knew they were going to have to be even more diligent about where they went and what they did. She hated it, but until this mystery about Paige was solved, she had no other choice. She shrugged her shoulders and said, "Okay, but can we look for agates on the way?" with a grin, and wrinkled up nose.

Marc grabbed her by the neck and jerked her closer, "Yeah, kiddo, we can search for agates." He then proceeded to plant a lingering kiss right over the saucy grin.

Sam was blushing as red as the tablecloth when he let her go. All three of the observers were smiling when she caught her breath and glanced at them. Even Paige was speechless for a change.

It was an unbelievably lovely day. The storm had cleared the air and left it sweet with the scent of the flowering plants. Sam threw her head back and took a deep breath, letting the sun warm her face. She was holding hands, Marc on her right, and Paige on her left, as they sauntered down the shore. How perfect it could have been if she could just sweep away the memory of last night.

Marc was silent, watching her attempt to relax. He was still absorbing his good fortune. Finally, she was letting him in, letting down her guard in front of him. If only they could find out who was stalking Paige, it would be perfect.

For now, he was enjoying the sight of her. Her long hair was down and flowing in the slight breeze, the sun glinted off her high cheekbones and tipped her nose. He couldn't resist. Tugging her hand to draw her closer he placed a soft kiss on her upturned lips. "Just because," he whispered.

As they approached the lodge, Sam and Paige stepped up onto the patio with their escort right behind them.

"Sam, it's been a long time!" As was usual for this family, Jessie ran forward and grabbed Sam in a big hug then took both of her hands and stepped back to look at her. "You don't look any different! Look at me - twenty pounds heavier, but you look like you did in school. That's not fair!"

"Being pregnant all of the time may have something to do with it." Marc dodged the jab his sister threw at him, then, swung her into a big hug. "Good to see you Jess, where's the rest of the gang?"

"They're out back by the garage. Jason is helping Dad fix up a kennel for the puppy, Jake, so he won't run away." Jessie knelt in front of Paige. "I bet you'd like to see the kids and the puppy wouldn't you?"

Paige nodded but clung close to her mother with one hand clutching her pants leg.

"Paige, this is an old friend of mine, and Marc's sister, her name is Jessie. She has three kids that I bet you'd like to play with." Samantha lifted Paige as Jessie rose so she would feel safer. Lately, she was really shy with strangers and Sam couldn't blame her.

Marc reached out and took Paige from Sam's arms. "C'mon, Pigeon. Let's go see what we can find to do while these two get caught up on the gossip."

Paige wrapped her arms around Marc's neck completely unaware of the scrutiny Jessie was giving them. Shifting Paige to one arm, Marc took Sam's chin between thumb and forefinger. He lifted her face and placed a soft kiss on her lips. This time both Jessie and Paige watched with interest.

"Just relax and visit with Jess. I won't let her out of my sight," he said softly. "We'll be out back getting acquainted. Knowing how talented that husband of yours is, I'm sure they need my expertise by now," he said to Jessie. He dodged another punch she threw at him and sauntered off bouncing Paige on his arm. Her giggles drifted back to the women watching them leave.

"My, oh my!" Jessie grinned at Sam. "What have you two been up to while I wasn't here to keep an eye on you."

For the second time that day, Sam blushed to the roots of her hair. "I swear Jessie, I didn't plan this, it just happened. I tried to tell him it wouldn't work. I'm such a mess right now. He deserves someone young and free from all of the baggage I carry." Tears formed in her eyes and her voice shook as she tried to explain.

"Sam, don't be embarrassed and don't feel that you aren't good enough for him. If I'm reading this right, I'm all for it. My brother has been in love with you since we were kids. If you two are happy, more power to you. From what I've gleaned, you've been through a nightmare, and I know Marc hasn't been happy either." She motioned to a patio chair she had just wiped dry. "Sit, we have a lot of catching up to do."

As they sat, Jessie leaned across the table and again took Sam's hand. "We're family, we always have been. If it's destined to be even closer I'm more than happy. Good luck with that brother of mine. Maybe if he has someone else to harass, he'll leave me alone for awhile," she said affectionately.

"The trouble is, my nightmare is still very real," Sam said.

"I know Sam, Mom and Dad have filled me in about some of it. I haven't talked to Marc yet, but by his actions something must have happened last night. Am I right?"

"Whoever it was, got into the house last night. He actually was in our house, Jessie! In Paige's bedroom."

"My God! No wonder you're a mess, and no wonder Marc is so protective this morning. I can't even imagine what I would feel if my kids were being stalked." Jessie gave a shudder at just the thought.

"It's just that I feel so helpless, so vulnerable to each and every noise, and so distrustful of every person I meet. I've taken to watching our guests so closely they probably think *I'm* a stalker."

"This can't go on, isn't there anything the authorities can do?"

"Seems not, as so far they haven't found any substantial clues, or any hard evidence at all. They probably think I'm nuts too."

"What do you mean too? If anyone has said they don't believe you, let me at them!"

"No, it's just that sometimes I question my own sanity. I search my mind for anyone that may have said something, or shown some sign, until I get a headache. I keep wondering who I've pissed off and can't come up with anyone. I wake up at night shaking with the dreams that have a shadowy figure in a hat and topcoat pulling Paige out of my arms."

"Oh Sam! I'm so sorry you have to go through this. From what Mom has told me you had a difficult marriage that ended tragically, and then your mother's problem, and now this, on top of it all. It just shows how strong you really are. I don't think I could have handled it nearly as well."

"Yes, you would have Jess. The truth is I don't even know where the strength comes from. It's just there when you know it has to be. There isn't any other option. You just dig down a little deeper and do what has to be done."

"I think what has to be done right now is for you to come meet the kids and Jason to get your mind off everything for awhile." Jessica pushed back from the table and stood up. Sam followed suit.

Sam, this is my husband, Jason, and this is Sherry - she's two. Robby is four, and the baby Michael is in the house with Mom taking a nap. Jason, this is an old friend, Samantha, from the resort next door. And Marc's *special* friend," she added with a gamine grin aimed at her brother.

Marc met the look with a raised eyebrow and a get-even look right back. "Okay just for that, you get to baby-sit Paige." He sent a questioning look at Samantha to check if that was okay with her before he continued. "We're going to wander over to my place for a bit."

They all looked over at the kids. The two older ones were taking Sherry for a walk and were being very protective. One on each side, they held her hands as she toddled along between them over the closely mowed lawn.

At that moment John stepped out of the garage with a pair of pliers in his hand. Seeing Sam, he stepped forward with his usual gusto and a welcoming, "Sampson, good to see you back!" He tossed the pliers to Jason, and Sam was once again enveloped in the familiar bear hug.

"Hands off my girl, old man!" Marc stepped forward as Sam was released. He caught his father's eye and read the relief transmitted there.

Both John and Peggy had felt the tension in the last few weeks. Hopefully, the fact that Sam was here again, with their son, was a good sign.

After Sam asked Paige if she would like to stay for a while and was assured she would like to, Marc and Samantha strolled off towards his old lodge hand in hand, deep in conversation.

It wasn't until they stepped up the worn wooden steps to the porch that Marc turned and swept Sam up into his arms. She clasped his neck in order to stabilize the both of them. With one hand, he managed to unlatch the heavy wooden door and elbowed it open. He carried her over the threshold, and with an impromptu waltz, whirled her over to the large, dark leather couch where he flopped down with her still in his arms.

Taking it from there, she held his face in her hands and planted a lingering kiss on ready lips.

Marc was overjoyed that she had finally made a first move on her own. It didn't take him long to warm up to the invitation. Cuddling her closer, and situating her more comfortably on his lap, he deepened the kiss.

Samantha lost all other thoughts and enjoyed the moment. She let the feelings soar while her breathing quickened. There were no objections when he stretched out on the wide couch and pulled her on top of him. This felt so right. For a long moment they just lay there, and she felt herself relaxing against the warmth of his body.

Then Marc's hands found the warm, bare skin under the purple tee shirt she wore. Adeptly unfastening her bra, his hands roamed to the silky skin on the sides of her breasts.

Sam's hands clutched his hair as she tendered moist, deep kisses. A low moan escaped her as his hands pushed her up far enough to cup the ivory globes. Feelings she hadn't felt in a long, long time overcame her, and she parted her legs to straddle him as she sat up and released his face to slowly lift his faded blue tee shirt and pull it over his head.

Marc raised his arms long enough to allow the removal of his shirt. He then lowered them to the bottom of her shirt and lifted both shirt and bra. His hands returned to the tempting mounds, caressing them as he watched her soft brown eyes turn slumberous. "You are so beautiful," he whispered.

"So are you," she whispered back, letting her hands roam over the sculptured muscles on his chest and her fingers tease the hardened nipples.

When he reached for the snap on her jeans she grabbed his hand. "Not today Marc."

He lifted his hands and pulled her back down on his chest. The feeling of her breasts on his bare skin was almost his undoing. "Any special reason why not?" he murmured, his face buried in the hair that was spread across his face.

"I just want you to be sure."

"Sam, I'm so sure I'm ready to burst!" he pushed her hair to the side so he could look into her eyes. "Samantha Stone, will you marry me?"

"Marc, are you sure you're sure?"

"I'm sure I'm sure. I'm just waiting for you to be sure."

His deep chuckle rumbled beneath her cheek, and she raised her head to look deep into those brown and green eyes so close to her. "I think I'm sure," she murmured. "I'm surprised at that fact, but yes, I'm sure. Yes, Marcus Hammond, I would love to be married to you."

"Yes!" The shout echoed through the old lodge. Marc grabbed Samantha by the back of her head and pulled her back into one hard, fast kiss then pushed her away. "Get dressed girl, I'm going to take you right back to the family and make you say it in front of witnesses."

They hastily donned their discarded clothing. Marc couldn't wait to announce the good news to his family. As they left the old lodge they took a quiet minute to enjoy the calm beauty of the water. The surface was so still that only the tiny circles from top-feeding fish broke the perfect reflections.

Marc pulled Sam in front of him, her back to his chest, and rocked her in gentle arms. "This will really be a home now," he whispered into her hair

"Home. That sounds so good," she whispered back and turned to lift her lips to his. It was awhile longer before they continued down the dusty road to join the rest of the family.

"Marc, can we talk to Paige first? I don't know if she understands too much of this. I don't want her to be upset. I know she loves you. I just think we should talk to her alone before we say anything."

"Whatever you think best. God, I love you!" They stopped walking long enough to enjoy another kiss under the scented branches of a twisted old cedar tree.

"I love you too!"

The couple floated on air as they made it back to the rest of the gang. They received a variety of looks as they joined the others, sitting around the kitchen table having lunch. Paige was standing next to the high chair and was watching intently as Jessie spooned cereal and applesauce into Michael's rosebud mouth.

The aroma from the large pan of lasagna and bowl of garlic bread on the table were tempting, but the couple had other things on their minds. The speculative looks from the adults became even more perplexed when Marc scooped Paige up and they stepped back outside without a word to the observers.

They sat at the same table that Jessie and Sam had left a short while ago; Marc kept Paige on his lap. Samantha pulled a chair close to them. "Pigeon, I have a special question to ask you. I want you to think about it really hard; then I want you to tell me the truth about what you're thinking. Will you do that for me?"

"Sure Marc! I'm really good at questions! I know the answer to lots of questions Mommy asks. Don't I, Mommy?"

"You're a very smart little girl, now listen to what Marc is going to say."

Marc boosted her onto the table in front of him so he could look into her eyes. "Pigeon, we're good friends aren't we?"

"You're my bestest friend in the whole world Marc."

"What would you feel about Mommy and I getting married, then I would be your daddy?"

"I had a daddy once, didn't I, Mommy?"

At the nod of her mother's head, Paige's little face lost its glow and a troubled look came into her eyes. "Sometimes Daddy wasn't very nice, was he Mommy?"

Marc's sharp glance towards Samantha captured the exact haunted look that echoed her daughter's. Realization hit him at once. It only took a few words out of the mouth of a child to paint a picture. Now, he knew what he had suspected and what she avoided talking about. Now, he could read the shadows in her eyes. Now, he understood her reluctance to let herself love again.

He closed his eyes and took a calming breath before he opened them and looked into Sam's troubled face. Their gazes locked and held for an unending moment. Her eyes told him she now knew he understood, while his begged her to believe it would never be like that again.

He turned to face the child in front of him. "Paige, do you think I'm nice? Do you think if I were your daddy I would be nice?"

"You're nice now. If you were a daddy, would you still be nice?" A chubby little hand came out and touched his face.

"I promise you and I promise your mommy that I will always be nice. I would never do anything to make Mommy sad, ever again. I love her, and I love you, and I want to be with both of you forever and ever. We would all live at my place. You know where we had the fish dinner? You like my cooking, you said you did, I remember." Marc smiled, winked and tickled her ribs as he reminded her. "And guess what, you could help pick out a new bedroom, all for yourself."

The adults watched as Paige pondered the question. She glanced at her mother. "I really would like a daddy. Michael and Bobby and Sherry have a daddy. He's nice to them and he built a really nice doggie house." She shifted her gaze to Marc with a sly look gleaming in her sparkling brown eyes. "Can you build a doggie house?"

Both Sam and Marc burst out laughing. "I think I'm being maneuvered here," Marc stated the obvious. "And just why would we need a dog house, Pigeon?"

"Maybe we could get a puppy too?" Paige questioned, her big brown eyes imploring. "And if you're my daddy could I have a baby brother too?"

Again the couple burst into laughter. "Your mother might have a little more say about that request," he added, but the thought was very appealing to him also.

"Well, have you thought about it? What do you think of the idea?" Marc was watching Paige's face intently, searching for a clue to what she was thinking.

She put one tiny finger up to her cheek, tipped her head sideways, and after a long moment said. "I thought about it and I would like it if Mommy and I married you. I would like you for a daddy, forever and ever."

Another "Yes!" escaped Marc, and he pumped his fist in the air before he grabbed his soon-to-be daughter and held her tight. His eyes caught Sam's and he was overwhelmed as tears formed and then fell, trickling down her cheeks as she covered her mouth with trembling hands.

He reached over with one hand and pulled her face into his shoulder. They shared an emotional moment before Paige started squirming. "Can I tell Bobby and Sherry I'm goin' to have a daddy?"

"Yes, Pigeon, you can be the one to tell them. Besides, all of a sudden I'm starving and that lasagna smells too good to be ignored."

The next couple of hours were filled with congratulations and good wishes. Mary and George were called and the news was a relief to them also. Maybe now Samantha could have the tender love and support she deserved. Maybe now the shadows would leave those beautiful, expressive eyes.

Samantha had put it off as long as she could. Today she was going to take Paige in to the school and enroll her in kindergarten. There was no way she could get out of it, and secretly hoped that the structure and safety of the school would be what Paige needed right now. She had met with the principal earlier and was assured that no one could get to her daughter unless they were completely vetted by personnel.

There were only three weeks left before school started so this was inevitable. For some reason it was even harder than leaving her at the daycare in the city. Then, Paige was unaware of the dangers that were possible. Now, she was fully aware of the stranger-danger she had only heard of then.

They entered the school office hand in hand. Because Paige hadn't been enrolled in a school before, the paperwork was simple. After they left the office a volunteer took them around the school and they ended up in the classroom Paige would be in for the following year.

This room was filled with most of the rest of the class. They were having a meet-the-teacher day, and noisy kids and chatting parents were partaking of some cupcakes and Kool-Aid. Paige's eyes lit up as she stood next to her mother.

One of the mothers noticed them and beckoned them to the table. Sam immediately recognized her. She was Kathy Garner who was working as a housekeeper at the resort. Sam knew she had children that her husband watched on the weekends when Kathy was working. They hadn't known their daughters would both be enrolling in the same class, and it was a pleasant surprise to both of them.

"Hi Sam, this is my daughter, Becky. Sit here and have some snacks with us," she gestured towards the pint-sized chairs sitting around the table. Sam gave her a quizzical look and raised one eyebrow. "I know, but if I can fit, you can fit," Kathy said.

The remainder of the afternoon was spent getting to know the rest of the parents, and the children. Paige was having a ball with all of the art supplies and puzzles that were available. It seemed her new best friend was Becky, because whatever one did the other was right along side of her.

"They really are getting along well aren't they?" Kathy mentioned to Sam. "This is the first time Becky's been able to meet kids her own age. There are a few neighbors though, with kids that are a little older or a little younger."

She turned and hesitated a second before continuing. "Becky has a birthday next Tuesday. Do you think Paige could come? I know it's kind of last minute but the neighbor kids are coming for a little party and I know Becky would like it if someone she's going to go to school with could come. It might help them both get through the first days if they had a friend there."

Samantha was torn. Should she stay protective or should she let Paige go to the birthday party? The answer was thrust upon her when the little girls, hand-in-hand, came to her.

"Can Paige come to my birthday party?" Big blue eyes implored, as the words were spoken.

Big brown eyes also begged as Paige simply said, "Please?"

It was a hard decision but Sam didn't let it show. She didn't feel like explaining their problems here in front of a room full of people. Her eyes met Kathy's.

"She'll be fine, I promise. We're having a barbecue in the back yard. It's fenced in so the kids can't get to the street."

"Okay, I guess." She said reluctantly. "How long would it last?"

"We're going to start about two in the afternoon, then go until they run out of things to do, and eat. We'll probably be done by five o'clock. Will that work for you?"

"That'll work, I'll bring her and pick her up. Thanks for the invitation." Sam worked her way out of the mini-chair and stood, shaking the cramps out of her legs.

Samantha was quiet all the way home, questioning her decision.

Paige, on the other hand, was full of chatter and was bouncing in her seat at the idea of going to a party. It was her animation that set Sam's mind at ease. She hadn't seen her daughter this excited about anything in a long time, too long of a time.

Chapter Eleven

Samantha thought she would sit and stew the whole time Paige was gone, but she got immersed in her work and the time flew by. She had checked on the guests to make sure they had everything needed to make their stay comfortable. Then she started on the bookwork that was so hard to do when Paige was constantly interrupting her.

Now, she looked at the clock on her desk and was surprised to see she only had fifteen minutes before she had to pick Paige up. She knew she could make it if she left right away, and was further surprised when she stepped outside and noticed the darkening skies. "Just what we need, another storm," she muttered.

As she arrived she noticed several partygoers walking home with their hats and gift bags clutched in their hands. "Right on time," she thought. She continued up the paved walk and knocked on the door.

Kathy answered the door with a questioning smile on her face. "Hi Samantha, what's the matter? Did Paige leave something here?"

"Leave? What do you mean leave? I'm here to pick her up."

The panic in her voice struck Kathy, and terror replaced the smile on her face. "Didn't you send her grandmother to pick her up?"

"Her grandmother? No! Her grandmother is home with my dad. I just left them at the resort."

"But Sam, a woman came and told me she was her grandmother and that you told her she was supposed to pick her up! She called you by name. Her exact words were, 'Samantha got busy at the resort and asked me to pick Paige up.' She knew your names, she knew about the resort."

"And you let her take her? I told you I would pick her up! How could you possibly let her go with someone you didn't know?"

"I did ask Paige, and she said, "Yes, that's Nana."

"Nana! You're sure she said Nana?"

"Yes, I'm sure. Samantha, is something wrong? You're as white as a sheet."

"Something wrong! Something wrong! Damn it all! My daughter has just been abducted and you ask, is something wrong?"

"Abducted! Oh my God!" Kathy almost collapsed before she caught herself, then ran to get the telephone and quickly dialed 911.

Within minutes the street was flooded with police cars. Sam had taken that time to make quick calls to Marc and to her parents from her cell phone. Marc and Mary arrived as the police were questioning Sam in Kathy's living room.

"What makes you think it was your ex-mother-in-law? Did you see her?"

"No I didn't see her but Paige called her 'Nana'. That's the only person she ever called that name."

One of the younger officers started to say, "But surely her grandmother" - when he was cut off by a senior official that had identified himself as Sergeant Peterson.

"Where does her grandmother live?"

"They lived in Burnsville the last I knew. I haven't heard from them in a long time."

"What kind of a car did she drive?"

"The last one I saw her drive was a white Ford, I don't remember what model."

"Do you have the grandparents telephone number?"

"It's on my cell phone."

"Here's what I want you to do. I want you to call and ask for your mother-in-law. If she answers we know it isn't her." Sergeant Peterson was very precise in his instructions.

Sam's hands were shaking as she opened her phone and located the number. She dialed then reached for Marc with her free hand while she waited. He stepped forward and put his arm around her shoulders.

"Jack, hello, this is Samantha." She waited for a second. "I know it's been a long time. Jack, could I talk to Sally for a minute?" Another long moment went by while she listened. "How long has she been in Iowa?" Her eyes flew to meet Sergeant Peterson's sharpened gaze. He beckoned her to give him the phone. "Jack, I have someone here that wants to talk to you."

"Hello Mr. Stone, this is Sergeant Peterson from the Shorecrest Police Department. We need to talk to your wife. I understand she isn't there. What kind of a car is she driving? No, as far as we know she hasn't been in an accident. What is the license plate number? What is your address?" He was busy scribbling notes on a pad. "Mr. Stone, there will be a police officer at your door momentarily. They will explain the situation and you can give them more information. No, I can't tell you more right now. You will be informed shortly." The sergeant flipped the phone shut and handed it back to Sam, "She's driving a light brown Chevrolet," he said in a grim voice. That's the description of the car you gave us on the Fourth of July wasn't it?"

"Oh my God! That's right. Jack said she's been in Iowa taking care of her sister all summer. They've kept in contact by cell phone."

"That will be easy to check, I've got a lot of work to do right now. We'll get out an APB and Amber Alert. We'll have the Highway Patrol watching the highways. You can go back to the resort and someone will be sent out there to stay until this is settled. Don't do anything on your own!" he warned.

Kathy had ushered her family out as soon as the police had arrived. She, however, had stayed in the background to answer the questions asked of her. Samantha noted the anguish on her face, as they got ready to leave.

"Kathy, it's not your fault. I should have explained the situation before leaving her. It's just that we were trying to keep things normal until we figured out what was going on. I'm sorry to disrupt your family on Becky's birthday."

"Keep me posted Sam, and let me know if there's anything else I can do." She stepped forward to give Sam one quick hug and turned to Marc. "Take care of her, too," she said as she glanced at the pale and shaking Sam.

Marc just nodded.

The weather broke for the worse during the ride home. As if it wasn't a bad enough evening to begin with, the rain pelted so fast the windshield washers couldn't keep up so the driving had to be slowed to a crawl. Marc drove Samantha, and Mary followed in Sam's car. No words were spoken; there just wasn't anything to say.

Sam was immersed in her own tragic thoughts. How could she have missed the possibility that it could have been Rocky's family? Now it was clear why they had become estranged. From the extent of the plans, Sally must have been planning this for a long time. She would swear, from the tone of Jack's voice, that he didn't know anything about it. He believed his wife to be in Oskaloosa, Iowa, taking care of a widowed sister that had broken her leg.

They were sitting in George and Mary's kitchen; Marc was talking to his parents on the phone, filling them in on the afternoon tragedy, when Deputy Cullen arrived.

He accepted the coffee they offered and all were again at the table when he received a call on his radio. Meanwhile John and Peggy had arrived, and they all watched him with interest as he stood and walked away while listening to the message.

After a short conversation he returned. "That was the sergeant. He said they checked out the car you described. It's licensed to Sally Stone, and it was reported as having been seen at a resort across the lake. The resort has been closed for years. That's why, when one of his officers noticed a car in the driveway while on his normal patrol of that area, he stopped to check it out. He didn't see anyone around but he did put it in his report. That was early this summer. He said he has since seen it on that road but there was nothing suspicious that drew any more attention."

Marc and Sam looked at each other simultaneously. They both rose at the same time.

"No!" Their movement triggered a response from the deputy. "I have orders to keep you here!"

"We're going! You can stay, or you can come with us, but *we are going!*" Marc helped Sam into her jacket and grabbed her hand as they headed out into the pouring rain.

It was a good thing Marc had brought his pickup truck. The dirt roads were turning to slippery mud and the rain continued to pour.

The deputy decided it was better to lead them to the area and they followed, the flashing lights glaring off the sheets of rain on the windshield.

As they approached the resort, they saw all sorts of law enforcement cars congregated with lights flashing on all of them. They parked behind the deputy, on the side of the road. The driveway to the abandoned resort was packed with cars and personnel.

One of the officers had a screaming woman by the arm; she was struggling to pull away. Sam recognized her at once and flew out of the car with Marc close behind her. As they approached, the officer pulled the woman's arms behind her back and cuffed her. Gray hair was drenched and stringing over the ranting face, but Samantha had no trouble recognizing her.

"Sally, what have you done? Where is Paige? What have you done with Paige?"

"What do you care? You don't deserve her! She's mine! She's all I have left of Rocky! She looks just like Rocky did when he was little! If you had made Rocky happy he wouldn't have died! Everything is all your fault!" The more she screamed the more demented she became. "If I hadn't come back here to pick up my stuff, we'd be gone, and you would have never found us! She would never have got out of the car and ran!"

Sam turned to the nearest officer and screamed. "Where is my little girl? Do you have her?"

"No! Not yet. We found evidence that this woman has been using one of the abandoned cabins. There are also receipts from several motels in the area that she has stayed in part of the time. We even found a clown costume. But we didn't find your daughter. This woman was outside in the rain looking through the brush when we apprehended her! She swore she didn't know anything about any little girl but we found this in her car." He pulled a crumpled party hat and a paper bag of treats out and showed her.

"Marc! She's here! I know she's here!"

"I know Sam, but there are people looking all over the area." Suddenly, Marc had an idea and went over to the lead officer.

After a brief conversation, the officer called all of the law enforcement people to him and instructed them, "Shut the lights off, get in your cars, and leave. Just wait down the road a ways until I give the word. This gentlemen thinks he can find the girl on his own."

Sally was escorted into the back of one of the squad cars and they all, one by one, shut off the flashing lights and left. More than one giving Sam and Marc questioning looks.

When the lights were gone and the crackling radios silent, Marc and Samantha stood quietly in the darkness. They slowly walked through the drizzling rain to the back of cabins.

"Pigeon? Pigeon, are you out there?" Marc's voice was loud but gentle. "Pigeon, you know I'm the only one that knows you by that name. It's safe for you to come out now. This is Marc, you know it's me, remember our secret name?"

"Paige, Mommy's here too." Sam's voice shook with fear as the silence continued to envelope them. She was almost afraid to breathe for fear she would miss any sound over the dripping of rain from the overhead canopy.

"Marc? Mommy?" The weak voice could barely be heard but both adults looked at each other to verify that the sound was real.

They slowly started in the direction of the voice. "Pigeon, speak a little louder so we can find you."

Once again they heard, "I'm in here." They turned to an overturned wooden barrel that had been abandoned next to a rotting woodpile. As they bent, a drenched little girl flung herself at them.

Tears couldn't be discerned from the lingering raindrops as the sopping wet trio embraced in the dripping forest.

"Let's go home. Now that we know who was causing all of the trouble, we won't ever have to be afraid again," Sam assured her daughter.

The police cars were still lined up dark and silent as the pickup approached them. Marc stopped and got out to assure them that they had found their daughter. One last look at the sullen woman in the back seat of the squad car, and he returned to his future, waiting for him to take them home.

Chapter Twelve

The past weeks had been the happiest of Samantha and Paige's life. Paige started school and loved it. Samantha got through the hectic Labor Day week at the resort and found time to relax once in awhile. George and Mary were once again involved with the business of restoring Pine Shores to its original beauty. It had been a traumatic summer, but now the brilliant leaves of autumn brightened the world. The air had a crisp snap to it that brought a rosy glow to cheeks that were tanned by the summer sun.

There had been many family debates, in which Paige had been included, to go over why Sally had done what she did. Sam and Marc thought that if it were discussed out in the open, Paige would be more open to talking about what her feelings were.

It appeared to be working. She still talked about how she got out of the car and ran, when her grandmother went into the cabin to pick up the damaging evidence of the clown outfit she had left there. She insisted on going back to see the barrel that she had hidden in, and once again crawled into it to show them how she fit, and told them how quiet she had been.

The courts, law enforcement, and mental health experts, were still busy with the aftermath. Sam was sure it would be a long time before it was all settled. She found it hard to feel sorry for Sally, no matter what she'd been through. She did, however, feel sorry for Jack who was drawn into a mess that was none of his own making. Maybe someday he could meet his granddaughter again, but Samantha just couldn't talk to him yet.

Today, however, was filled with only happy thoughts. Jessie, Sam, and Paige were in Sam's bedroom dressing for a very important occasion. Today they were getting married. At least that is what Paige insisted.

"Mommy and I are marrying my new daddy," is what she had been telling everyone.

She had conceded to wear a pink and white, frilly confection of a dress. Lots of layers made the skirt stand out like the petals of a pink rose. She turned and admired herself in the full-length mirror.

The wedding was being held in the new lodge at the Hammonds' Wilderness Resort. Only family, and a few close friends were invited.

"Okay Paige, you look ready, and you look beautiful. Now go downstairs and wait with Grandma. And stay clean!" Sam admonished.

After her daughter left, Samantha turned to Jessie. "How's Marc? Does he say anything to you? Do you think he really knows what he's getting into?" Insecurity once again hit Sam. Could she live up to the expectations of being the wife she knew Marc deserved?

Jessie looked at her and saw the lack of confidence in Sam's worried eyes. "Sam, sit here," she said, indicating a stool by the vanity. As Sam perched on the stool, Jessie stood behind her and started smoothing some wayward strands of hair before she placed the lacy band that had pink and white flowers woven into it. The pink baby roses matched the pastel silk suit that Sam was wearing.

"Now just close your eyes," Jessie instructed.

Sam was curious. What was her friend up to now? However, she did as she was told as Jessie continued to adjust and fasten the headpiece.

"Sam, just stop and think back to when we were kids. Who was always there to help you when you needed help? Who was always willing to go fishing, to start the motor, to dig worms, or catch minnows for bait?"

Samantha was beginning to realize where Jessie was going with this. Her mind did return to the past and as close a friend as Jessie had been for girl talk, that wasn't what came foremost to her mind.

Jessie said no more as Sam's memory took her back to simpler times. How many times had she searched out Marc when she wanted to have a serious talk? Even though younger he had always been sensible and responsible. Now she realized how he had always been able to read her moods, know what she was thinking, and always knew what to say or what not to say to make her feel better. She had always felt comfortable and safe when he was close.

At the time, she had not associated the closeness in a romantic way but now considered the possibility that the love they now shared was being built those many years ago. Marc assured her over and over that he had loved her for years. Now, Jessie, who had observed it all, affirmed it.

"Thanks, Jessie. I needed that. I thought it was the groom that was supposed to get cold feet the day of the wedding."

"No chance of that happening! I know my brother. I don't think he slept all night and was chomping at the bit this morning. Why do you think he sent me over here to hurry you up?"

The weather was perfect. It was so nice in fact, that the wedding was held on the patio. Occasionally a golden leaf from the clump of birch fluttered down. Nature's own confetti was covering the ground. The shadows were gone, shouldered aside by the brightness and warmth of the autumn sun.

Paige didn't understand a lot of the pledges her mother and new dad were making, but she did understand when the minister said, "I now pronounce you man and wife. You may now kiss the bride."

The soft, lingering kiss was interrupted by a little voice asking, "Are we married now?"

Marc gazed into Sam's dark brown eyes and saw the look he had waited so long for. "I love you," he whispered then reluctantly let her go long enough to pick Paige up. "Yes baby, *we* are married now."

"Can I call you Daddy now?"

"I would be very, very happy if you would call me Daddy." Marc turned to Sam for another quick kiss before they turned to face the observers, several with tears in their eyes.

"Come on now! Only smiles from now on," he encouraged. "You remember what we talked about, Paige?"

"I remember! We can have lunch, then I get to have a sleepover with Sherry and Michael and Bobby at my new Grandpa and Grandma's house!"

The newlyweds were barely aware of what that lunch consisted of, only of what lay ahead. They only stayed long enough for appearance's sake, then thanked everyone and kneeled to say goodbye to Paige.

"Where are you going?" she asked.

"Remember, we told you - Mommy is going to have a sleepover at my house." He turned to smile at Sam. "Forever and ever."

Marc and Samantha hugged Paige and promised to see her in the morning. As they walked down the narrow road between the houses, they turned one last time when they heard a little voice yelling at them.

"Remember what you told me," Paige was shouting. "Don't stay awake all night talking!"

"I can promise that, Paige!" Marc shouted back, which brought laughter from the rest of the wedding party.

They ended up running as soon as they were out of sight. When they reached the door, Marc once again swept her up and carried her over the threshold. This time, though, he didn't stop at the couch but headed for the curved stairway that led to the bedrooms in the loft.

"Now," she whispered as he laid her across their bed. Her shaking hands began to loosen his tie and unbutton his shirt. "I'm sure, I'm really, really sure. I love you with all of my heart."

"At last," he whispered. "It seems like I've waited a lifetime. My best friend in all-of-the world is now my wife. I will love you forever."

NORMANDALE COMMUNITY COLLEGE
LIBRARY
9700 FRANCE AVENUE SOUTH
BLOOMINGTON, MN 55431-4399